RUNES OF MORTALITY

A DEMON'S FALL SERIES

G. BAILEY

Runes of

Mortality

Book Two

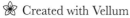 Created with Vellum

Death should have been the end, but instead, it's the start of my revenge…and they won't even see me coming.

Evie survived a trip to Hell, literally, to find herself somewhere even more dangerous—with the angels. Angels who do not want to let her leave, not without paying a price for the life they saved.

Angels. Demons. Protectors and more secrets than one world should hold. Who can Evie trust when everything is a lie? When it's time for the assassin to return and claim what is hers, who will be on her side?

18+ Reverse Harem romance.

For the brilliant, inspiring man who brought me up. I miss you every day.

AZI

THE PORTAL BURNS INTO EXISTENCE, the pressure of going to the one place I knew was impossible to ever travel to without a great cost burning through my thoughts. The cost doesn't cross my mind, not even for a second, as I make the portal larger and feel the massive drain on my power. I growl low as sweat drips down my head, and finally, the portal breaks the barrier to a place I never thought I would go to. I jump through the portal, landing on top of a white brick house as I take in everything. A screaming angel draws my attention behind me where a white-haired angel is running away from an army of souls, screaming her head off. My heart catches in my throat as Evie runs around a wall, a stone in her hand as the army of souls is just behind her. *What the hell is she doing?* The blonde angel trips, falling flat on her face in the grass. Evie picks up a fallen branch, spinning around and swinging it at a soul as I jump off the house and start running towards her. I run around a house just in time to see small black wings appear on her back, and she flies into the air, only to be caught around the foot by a soul. The souls slowly pull her down as I run, jumping over walls to get to her in time.

"Evie!" I shout as more souls get hold of her, and I call my fire into my hands. I run and jump right into the middle of the souls where Evie disappeared, praying that she will survive this. *I can't exist without her.*

Chapter One

EVIE

"COME UP OFF THE GROUND. The outside is not safe for our kind. Let us go to my home," the angel says smoothly as I stare at my wings. *My wings. I have freakin' wings.* I repeat the same things in my mind as I reach over and smooth a hand down my left wing. I can feel the soft feathers under my fingers, and my wings flutter gently. Can I fly? I wonder about it for only a second before I realise I have bigger problems. *Like where the hell I am, for one.*

"Child, we must leave," the angel demands. I turn to look at him and stand myself up, only to nearly trip at the new weight of the wings on my back. They aren't that big and stop at my hips, but they weigh a lot. The angel holds his hands on his hips as he waits for me to say anything.

"I am not a child, and I want to know where the hell I am. I need to know how quickly I can get back to earth," I snap, and I look at my wings once more. "And who the hell gave me wings? I am no angel, so someone made a big mistake there."

"That is a complicated answer, one I cannot tell you here. It is not safe. The souls are leaking into the third layer of Hell, and every night, we get attacked," he explains, and I almost laugh at his lie.

"That's impossible. The three guards of the third layer would never let souls in. They can't even get to the second layer!" I exclaim, calling the angel out on his bullshit and wrapping my arms around me as I suddenly notice I'm naked as I chat to the strange, older angel. I think he is old anyway, I'm not that sure. His long white hair makes him look aged, as well as those white eyes. The white clothes aren't helping him look younger, that's for sure. I stare at the angel for a second, wondering how it is even possible an angel is alive. They are all meant to be dead. The ones I've heard about were crazy enough to try and destroy earth and paid for their mistake. I should be on guard with this angel and find a weapon as soon as possible. And some damn clothes before my butt freezes off.

"They do not know about what truly happens in

the layer they are meant to protect. No one truly knows what happens in Hell anymore because there are no royals," he says, his tone clearly frustrated. When I just stare at him, not believing one word of his crap, he points a finger at a small building in the distance. "That is my house. I am going there, and you can come if you wish. I won't force you but only suggest that being out here isn't a good idea." With that lovely statement, he walks off, and I'm stood alone, watching him go. I don't know the angel or anything about angels in general other than they are crazy. I literally don't have a clue what powers he could have.

I run my hands over my scars without thinking about them, and suddenly, I'm remembering Erica's victory face as I died and feeling nothing but over-whelming anger. I am going to kill that bitch when I get to her. I also remember the Protectors shouting for me as I died, and that Hali is now alone. Azi is captured, but I doubt even his brothers can keep him long, and when he escapes, he will go for Hali. At least I hope so. I can't stand the thought of her being alone with Erica, who will no doubt kill her or send her to the witches to spite me. I need answers and to get the hell out of here quickly, and it looks like the old angel is all I have for now. Let's hope I don't have to kill him if he is as crazy as his relatives must have been.

I run after the angel, looking down at the ground, which I think is actually a white cloud and feels so soft as I run on it. Everywhere just looks white, full of clouds, and there isn't anything other than the small white house I get to. *What the hell is this place? If it is Heaven, then someone made a big mistake.* I slow down as I get to the house, which looks extremely old, made of white stone and has an ancient Greek feel to it. The angel has left the white door open for me, but I don't go in straight away as I hear a loud unrecognisable noise. I sharply turn around and see a massive group of souls in the distance, running towards something I can't see. The angel was telling the damn truth. I carefully walk through the door, not trusting the angel. He might be leading me into a trap, but I know he is right about being outside. That is way too many souls to kill.

"Shut the door, won't you, child? We don't want to get the souls' attention. They never come this way, but let's not test it tonight," the angel asks with a long huff. I look over to where he is sitting on a chair, in front of a white fire which is inside a white stone fireplace. The fire burns pure white, and there is no wood, stones or anything holding the fire. It is just floating in there like a creepy ghost. I pull my eyes away when the angel clears his throat, and I shut the door behind me quietly. He is right, but I'm not admitting that to him.

"There are clothes over there. They belonged to a friend, and she is smaller than you. They may be tight," the angel says as he points to a small table next to a wooden, clearly unused, bed on the other side of the room. I ignore his comment as I go over, picking up the white dress that is designed to be held up by your boobs I think. I pull it up, and it rests nicely, not bothering my wings which knock into the bed, causing a slight bit of pain. Great, this is not what I need right now. I glance around the room, searching for any weapons and finding nothing. There are no plates, glass or anything other than a chair that I could use to make damage if this angel attacks me.

"Shit," I say, nearly tripping again as I attempt to turn around. The wings spread out, and I just stare at them in exasperation. I did not want them to do that.

"You can put the wings away until you've learnt how to control them," the angel says, sighing loudly like I am an annoying child or something to him.

"How?" I ask.

"Say 'alis abierunt' while thinking of your wings disappearing," he informs me, and I close my eyes, repeating his words and thinking of myself with no wings. I don't expect the wings to be gone when I open my eyes, but they are, only a little black dust left on the floor behind me even suggests they were ever there.

"How do I get them back?"

"You simply think of them, and they will appear. I will help you learn how to fly and balance in time, and you eventually will not even need to think or speak words. Your mind and wings will connect to protect you," he clarifies, his white hair hiding his face from me as he rests back.

"In time? I'm not staying here long, buddy," I reply, and he laughs low.

"If you find a way out that none of us have ever done, that will be impressive. Whoever you are, you are stuck here and lucky I was here to help. No angels leave the town, and I only came to check what the noise was," he tells me, and I pause, panicking a little. I need to leave. Hali needs me, and that bitch of a sister needs to know why she can't kill me and get away with it. Honestly, I'd rather be dead than stuck here, at least I could haunt her ass.

"Where are we?" I ask quietly, not really wanting the answer. I have a feeling it isn't good or escapable. The angel turns his head, so our eyes meet, and entwines his fingers together on his lap as he sits back. He looks strange to me. His features are almost perfectly aligned, and his skin seems to glow constantly.

"You might want to sit down," he replies smoothly, his voice is commanding and somehow nice at the same time. The angel still freaks me out, but I doubt he wants to kill me. He would have attacked me by now, and he clearly thinks I'm like him. I slide into the wooden chair opposite him, still keeping myself on guard just in case. I don't trust the motives of any stranger that just helps random people without wanting something in return. I know there are good people out there, but it's like finding a needle in a haystack.

"We are stuck in the stars on the third layer of Hell. Angels cannot die in Hell, it is impossible to die in a place that has no connection to the place we come from. A demon figured out killing us here would trap us, so there was a great war. I am too young to know all the details as I have only been trapped here twenty-six years, but the other angels talk," he says.

"You're saying I'm an angel?" I ask, trying not to smile. *You have to be kidding me.*

"You're a half angel, of course," he tells me, and I just burst into laughter. That is the funniest thing I've heard in years.

"That's…well, there are no angels on earth anymore," I say once I've calmed down, and he is staring at me like I'm an idiot or something. "Therefore, my father couldn't have been an angel," I counter, though my argument is weak and stinks of denial. *Shit, I'm a half angel. What kind of messed up crap is this?*

"There were a few left on earth years ago. Angels who did not want to fight and had not lost their minds in war. There were three of us, and one of us must be your father," he says, looking away from me.

"Are they all here?" I ask, not knowing if I want to meet my father. Everything is too much at the moment. My mother was queen of the Protectors, and I was a child never meant to exist. I always knew that my parentage wasn't going to be a big happy answer, but it is still more than I could have ever expected. The way Erica talked of our mother, it's clear she hates her for having me. If I don't kill Erica the moment I see her, maybe I can get some more answers.

"No. I am the only one alive, and I never had a child who lived, before you even think to ask." He doesn't look my way as he speaks, so I have no idea if he is telling me the truth or not. "Who is your mother? I may know more then."

"I do not want to talk about that," I snap because it's not something I can cope with saying out loud yet. The angel finally stares at me for a second and nods in understanding.

"Fine. I have a gift, an ability to see into the past. I can search your mind and find the answer if you wish? I would very much like to know who you are. The angels left on earth, well they were like brothers to me," he explains to me. I go to say no when I pause, looking at my blue hair as I twirl it in my finger. This angel could show me what happened to my mother, what happened to make my hair turn blue…I could learn everything I have always wanted the answers to. I might need to know my past to challenge my sister when I get out of here, because there is no way she is telling me the truth about everything.

"Can I see the memories with you?" I ask.

"Yes, that is possible," he agrees.

"Fine, we have an agreement. What is your name?" I ask, knowing if I'm going to work with the angel, I might as well get to know some details.

"Danike, yours?" he replies smoothly. Weird ass name, but then angel names might all be like that.

"Evie. Now where can I get a weapon and a bacon sandwich?" I ask, needing my favourite things urgently.

"We do not have weapons here, and we are vegetarians," he answers. *Oh god, people that don't eat bacon.*

"You have to be kidding me," I groan and rest back in my seat. *Heaven, Hell or whatever this place is, it sucks.*

Chapter Two

EVIE

"ARE WE LEAVING YET?" I ask, feeling like the human kid from that movie that asks if we're there yet a million times over. Danike just raises a bushy white eyebrow at me before turning his head and he goes back to looking through a gap in the curtain. I've come to notice that angels do not sleep, or at least this one doesn't. Also, there is no meat to be seen anywhere, just lots of strange white fruits and vegetables that Danike tried to force feed me last night.

"You could do with learning a little patience, did your mother not teach you that?" he asks, his tone ringing with sarcasm.

"She is dead, and I was brought up on the streets. So, no," I dryly respond. Danike gives me a slightly sad-filled look, before looking back at the gap, and I'm glad he does. I don't need his sympathy, and he is going to see my past soon anyway. He suddenly straightens up and walks to the door, swinging it open and walking out. I follow him out, keeping a close eye on my surroundings and not seeing anything but clouds for miles. No souls to be seen, thank god.

"We must fly to get where we need," Danike says, looking me over, "which is going to be troublesome for a new one like you."

"Where are we going? You never explained anything," I ask, putting my hands on my hips and ignoring the "new one" comment.

"There is a safe haven for angels in the sky above us that the souls have not managed to get to. We need another angel's help to use my powers here. On earth, angel powers are boosted, but down here…it is not the same," he explains, clearing his throat. "Now, wings."

"Wings?"

"Yes. Get them out," he demands.

"I really don't feel like that's a bright idea. I cannot fly."

"Evie…you can't run from who you are and deny it. You are a half angel, half of one of the most powerful species in existence. If you learn how to control that side, you can get revenge on whoever killed you in Hell," he says.

"Fine," I reply, knowing he is right, and I can't avoid ever using the wings again. Closing my eyes for a second, I imagine my wings. I feel the weight of them on my back before I even open my eyes to see them spread out behind me. The feathers on them are black and soft looking, and it is really strange.

"To fly, spread your wings out and think of flying. It is that easy. Once you are up, just think of where you wish to go," he says, and his wings spread out, lifting him into the air. He floats with his wings flapping as he waits for me. *Come on, Evie, it's just flying. No big deal.* I look at my wings and think of them spreading out, which they do, and then I think of flying up in the air. My wings slowly flap, once and then twice, before they shoot me up into the air, and I keep going up. I scream as I keep flying up, and then start spinning in circles. I can't think straight as I try to make them stop in my mind, but nothing happens. *Fuck.*

"Slow down! Think of slowing down!" I hear Danike shout as the wind batters against my face, and I feel myself spiralling out of control. I think of slowly flying, balancing in the air, and I finally slow down, flying gently in a circle. I sway as I try to shake off the dizziness from all the spinning as my wings fly me around. A cold hand clamps on my arm, stopping me from flying in circles, and I follow the hand to see Danike flying next to me.

"Good. Now this way," he instructs and lets me go. I imagine myself flying slowly after him, and surprisingly it works. I fly right behind Danike as we turn left and then fly down a little. A massive cloud comes into view, and Danike flies right into it. I have nowhere else to go, so I follow him in, slowing my wings down a little in case there is anything to bump into. There is nothing but white cloud for a long time until I come out the other side and see a small village in a cloud. All the houses are white and ancient, there is white grass surrounding them and a water fountain in the middle. It looks like ancient Greece, at least the pictures I've seen online of it. There are even some statues of angels in the far distance near the bigger houses. I glance to my left as someone flies up to Danike, but her eyes stay on me. Another angel. She is stunning with long white hair and a white dress like mine on her. I bet this dress is hers. The angel is much shorter than we are, and she looks concerned as she glances at

Danike. Her wings are massive, even larger than Danike's and have a silver shine to them that matches her silver eyes.

"Who is she?" the woman asks, her question fearful and nervous.

"Evie. She appeared at the border last night. She doesn't know who her father is, but he must have been one of the last on earth. I need your help to remember her past," he replies just as I get to his side and think of my wings just floating me in place. Thank god it works, or I would look like an idiot falling.

"Does she know she is stuck here?" the angel asks. "She doesn't look like she is having a mental breakdown about being trapped forever."

"Yes, she knows and seems to think she can escape. I'm sure Evie will come to realise the truth soon enough," Danike replies smoothly.

"I am right here, and I am getting out of here," I state firmly, even if I don't have a clue as to how I'm going to accomplish that. The angel smiles at me, running her eyes over my body and back up again.

"Maybe she knows something we don't. Either way, this place is boring, and it will be fun to have someone new around. Come on then, Evie."

With that, she shoots down towards the houses in the blink of an eye. I have to learn how to move that quickly, it's awesome. Danike quickly follows after her, and I make my wings move, flying me down in the direction they went. I look around, seeing no one outside the houses, and everything is so still other than the sound of my wings moving as I get closer to the ground. *Where is everyone?*

I fly to the house that Danike and the angel land outside of, wondering how to land in the graceful way they do. I think about to how they landed, and know it can't be that hard. I think of landing on the clear patch of white grass I spot in front of the house, and my wings start to slow down. I land with a thud, rolling across the grass and feeling bruises everywhere, plus what I'm pretty sure is grass burns on my legs.

"Fucking hell," I mutter as I cough out some of the white grass in my mouth. Hearing someone laugh, I look up to see Danike and the angel watching me from the door, the angel bent over laughing with her hair covering her face. I try not to be completely intimidated by the very gorgeous woman as she laughs at me, but it's hard. If we were back home, I would likely make her a friend of mine. She is stunning, and I wonder if she has some kind of natural draw to her. It might be her power, for all I know. The odd thing is how the angel looks at Danike, like he has the drawing nature when he doesn't one bit. Danike doesn't even seem to notice her at all by the looks of it. Even the gorgeous women can't always get the guy it seems.

"Totally clueless, isn't she? I think I love it and her," the angel laughs even more. Even her laugh is beautiful, and I don't even like girls. *Dammit, I feel like the ugly duckling right now.*

"I believe her death in Hell unlocked her wings for the first time. Her father must never have met her to unlock them before," Danike muses. "I wonder if she will have any other powers."

"Well, I am looking forward to seeing who her father is. I bet it's Aniker, he was always a bit of a player after what you told me, and you said he loved demons. She is clearly half demon with that beautiful hair," the angel states, waving a hand at me. The blue hair, of course, is making her think I am a demon.

"I'm half Protector," I explain as I stand up, wiping grass off me and looking at my runes on my arms. I call my healing mark to heal the bruises forming everywhere, but nothing happens. I frown, wondering what the hell is wrong now. I tap the rune a few times, knowing it won't do anything, but it makes me feel better.

"Protectors have a small bit of angel blood, and this place makes you need a lot of power to do anything. Your powers will not work here even as a half angel," the angel informs me as Danike just strangely stares at me.

"Great! No bacon, no weapons and now no runes! This place is fucking fantastic!" I grumble, and the angel laughs.

"Why don't you come inside, Evie?" she asks. "I don't have any of those things, but I do have fruit freshly picked. It is lovely."

"What is your name?" I ask, avoiding rolling my eyes at the idea of anymore of their fruit. Choking some down last night was enough. I keep my eyes on Danike who looks like he has just seen a ghost or something as he stares at me. Did he not realise I was a Protector or something?

"Charmeine," she says, before opening her door and walking inside with Danike following right behind her after he snaps out of whatever trance he was in. I think of my wings disappearing, whispering the Latin phrase under my breath and watching my wings as they disappear this time.

They disappear into black smoke, leaving a little black dust that falls to the floor. I'm surprised it's not painful and that I can't feel the wings leaving at all.

"Evie?" I hear Charmeine shout for me. I look around at the ghost town once more before walking in the house, knowing I have plenty of questions I need the answer to. *Like if this was a place all the angels in Hell came to, where are they all?*

Chapter Three

"NOW, I am going to count to three, and if you don't speak quickly, I will rip your throat out," I growl, holding the whimpering demon in the air with my one hand. The demon shakes his head, still refusing to tell me what my brothers are up to. The demon is only young, with dark black hair and black eyes. I doubt his powers have even really come through yet as I bet he is about seventeen, and I have no intention of killing him…but I have to know what happened to get me here. One minute, the floor is falling through in my old home, no doubt a bomb of some sort by my brothers. The next thing I know, I'm waking up with what feels like the worst hangover as this demon drags me down the stairs of a basement. *Where the fuck is Evie and those damn Protectors? If anyone has hurt her, the world will burn for it.*

"One," I start, and he still refuses for a moment, until I start warming my hand up with fire. As his neck burns lightly, he screams and screams, wriggling to get free. Not that I am really hurting him. Not yet anyway.

"Okay!" he finally shouts, and I let him drop to the floor. The demon stares up at me, fear-filled eyes darting around the room as he rubs his throat with his hand.

"I haven't got all day," I snap, feeling impatient.

"They are kidnapping all your brothers and a few demon experimenters who work in a lab I don't know much about. I don't know what they are doing, I swear. My father only told me to lock you in here, and then you woke up early…" he squeaks the last part out. Shit, this is bigger than I thought. I need to find Evie and get Hali.

"You tell my brothers everything went fine. That I'm locked down here. Understood?" I tell him, rubbing at my arm where there are several cuts that are only just healing. *They took my blood, but why?* I storm out of the basement of cages, all of them empty, and call a portal, the need to find Evie the only thing on my mind.

I walk through the portal that leads me to an old, haunted house in the middle of New York City. My friend has lived here for centuries and never wanted to change the house, even as the high rises where built right next to it. It looks very odd in such a built-up city, but everyone knows a powerful demon lives here, and they aren't stupid. The door opens and Lamia steps out, watching me closely but not inviting me in. She never has in all the years I've known her. Lamia looks like an old woman, and she wears rags even though money is not a problem for her. She also uses this appearance to come across as weak and helpless when she is anything but. People walk down the street in front of me as I slide my hands into my pocket, keeping eye contact with Lamia.

"Azizi…what brings you to my door for the first time in hundreds of years?" she asks, her voice clear even though we are a far distance apart. I walk over to her house, stopping just outside her picket fence. I know I cannot step foot onto her land without paying a price, which many demons do not know. She smirks at me, knowing I wouldn't fall for her trap like many others.

"I need your assistance," I answer.

"An overlord needs my help? My, my…how things have changed," she muses, laughing low.

"I helped you once. You owe me, and demons always pay their debts," I remind her.

"This is true. Time moves so quickly these days, I forget the past and my debts at times," she says, and I understand that. Lamia walks down the steps of her house, lowering her hood, and her empty eyes meet mine. Her eyes have no pupil, nothing but an off-white colour glazed across them. The street goes silent, and I look around to see she has frozen all the people walking down the street, the cars and everything. Nothing moves.

"How can I assist you?" she asks.

"Find someone. Her name is Evie, and she is the deadly assassin, helper of demons—"

"Salvatore. I have heard her name whispered everywhere recently. Many look up to her for the future," she says, her tone serious. "Many say she is the lost royal child of the Protector and she will be queen. Queen of the Protectors and demons."

"Then help me find her," I ask, thinking over her words. *She is fucking what?* I don't even have a clue what happened while I was out, but clearly a lot did. The queen of the Protectors? How can that even be possible? Her mother or father couldn't have been a royal. Lamia places her hands over her ears, and she nods to me. Her white eyes glow brightly for only a second. The light is dazzling and so pure, much like it is said her power is meant to be, pure and endless, though I don't always believe all the rumours. I wait for her to lower her hands after she seems like she is back from wherever she was.

"Salvatore cannot be found by me. I already know it, so will you. She has died in Hell," Lamia informs me, her voice cold and unfeeling. The shock rolls through me when I sense the truth in her words. Evie is gone, that's why I cannot feel her. That's why everything feels wrong.

"No," I shake my head, stepping back and feeling my anger take over. The floor starts melting as fire drips off my body, and my inner demon takes over. I can't even think, not wanting to fight him if she is gone.

"You must go to the Protectors if you wish for answers. They hold the key," Lamia says, snapping me out of it a little to look at her in confusion. My inner demon slides back into the mental cage I keep him in, and the fire slows down into little embers that drip off my skin onto the floor.

"Why would I care for anything if she is gone?"

I ask, but I remember Hali and know I have to save her before finding out what happened to Evie and destroying those responsible.

"Death is not the end for us all, overlord. You know this. I believe the Salvatore needs to return for her revenge soon. The Protectors are the key," she tells me, filling me with a little hope as she bows her head and whispers, "Sempiternum daemonum futurum oriri."

"Demons will rise," I repeat her words, but in English. Lamia means them in a show of respect as that's what they were always used for. Now demons only whisper the saying, not understanding where it came from. I bow my head before turning and walking down the street, where people are now walking around like nothing just happened. *Time to find those annoying Protectors and Hali.*

Chapter Four

EVIE

"COME IN, come in. I never see anyone these days, and never someone new!" Charmeine happily tells me, practically jumping on the spot as I walk into her house. Seems like falling out of the sky and spitting out grass has made her like me more. *Go figure.* Danike shuts the door behind me as I take in the simple room before me. There are two sofas, a fireplace much like Danike's, and a white fluffy rug in the middle of them. There is a kitchen with what looks like white apples in a bowl on the side and a small table and chairs. There are white flowers in vases everywhere, and the whole place feels like a cosy home.

"Why is everything white?" I ask.

"We don't actually know. See, I have only been up here for five hundred years and everything was white when I first came up. Not all the older angels like to talk, so it's hard to find things out," she says.

"How long have some of you been here?" I ask.

"Thousands of years," Charmeine says, her voice tainted with sorrow. "Most of them left have been here that long. Danike, my sister and I are considered outsiders."

"How many are alive here?" I ask.

"She asks a lot of questions, doesn't she?" Charmeine asks Danike rather than answering me.

"Unfortunately, yes," he says, rubbing his jaw as he watches me. "There are thirty-two angels alive here."

"That isn't a lot," I muse, walking around the room.

"Souls come…we cannot fight. We are not warriors like the angels that were on earth. We were sent to Hell to make peace with the demons…but we found only death instead," Charmeine tells me, her silver eyes locking on mine. I'm sure there is far more to it than that, but I'm not sure if I want to know more right now. I came here to see my past, not deal with the past of the angels.

"I want to see her past. That is why we are here," Danike tells Charmeine who nods, looking me over.

"Fine. It will hurt. Are you ready for that?" she asks carefully.

"Pain is just pain, and this time the pain will be for something. I have never known who my parents are, which has always stuck with me. I only just found out about my mother…and I do not have the answers I need yet about my father," I explain to her.

"I never knew my parents either, and I only got trapped here when I heard rumour my sister was trapped in the stars of Hell," she says sadly, somewhat making me like her a little bit more.

"Was she here?" I ask.

"Yes. My sister lives and will be back soon. She is much younger than us. Only a child when she was killed and came here. We are so very slow here that she is only a teenager now," she tells me and looks over at Danike. "We should start, the memory will knock you out for the day and drain me. I do not want to still be under when it gets dark."

"Understood. Lie next to me, Evie," Danike says, and walks into the lounge. He lies down on the fur rug, and Charmeine goes to kneel next to him. She looks up at me and pats the floor on her other side. I start to wonder if letting her put me to sleep is a good idea or not. I can't fight when I'm not awake.

"We will not hurt you. You are our kind, related to us in some way. We are the last of the angels, and we need to know who you are. You need to know who you are," Charmeine says kindly, and I know she has a point. I don't like the idea of being defenceless, but this is the only chance for the memories I need. I slowly walk across the room and lie on the floor next to her.

"You may see some of Danike's memories as his powers link you. It is normal," she tells me, and I nod once. Charmeine places a hand on both Danike's and my foreheads. Her touch is freezing cold as she starts chanting a language I do not understand. The room slowly fades away into a white light, a light that shines so bright that I cannot see anything but it as I can only hear Charmeine's chanting. When the light fades a little and the chanting disappears, I pull myself up and sharply turn around, seeing nothing but a white room with nothing in it. The room spins rapidly, causing me to fall over even as I try to keep up. I close my eyes as the room spins and spins, a scream ripping out of my throat as my hands go to my head.

"Open your eyes," Danike's voice comes to me, and as I do, the spinning suddenly stops. I see the gold fur rug I am seated upon first, spreading my fingers in it as everything stops blurring. I stand up quickly, pausing at the sight of a man leaning over a woman in her bed. The bed is huge, and the frame looks like it is made out of solid gold that is decorated in runes. There are gold coloured curtains, a solid gold dressing table and one beautiful painting on a wall. The painting is of a dark-haired woman kneeling on gold grass as a gold light blasts off her body.

"Open your eyes. I miss seeing the beauty in them, Eella," the man says softly, and I step closer, seeing that it is Danike, hidden in a white cloak. I don't recognise the soft tone in which he speaks to the woman he looks down at. The woman in the bed sharply sits up, wrapping her small arms around Danike's shoulders as they kiss, her long dark hair hiding her face from me. When she pulls back, I see her runes on her face, her blue eyes and her long black hair. Her large pregnant stomach comes into view, and I just know who she is. It is like finding someone you have always known is just there but never seen. She is my mother.

Chapter Five

EVIE

THE ROOM SPINS rapidly as I stare at my mother. One minute, I am watching Danike kiss my mother once again, and then I am in the same room, but it is on fire. A woman's hand hangs off the bed, her hanging arm and shoulder is the only thing I can see. I slowly walk over, seeing the piles of blue dust on the floor. Dead demons. Dozens of them. I swallow the nervous feeling in my throat making me feel sick as I get to the bed. My whole body goes cold as I see my mother lying on the bed, holding a baby to her chest that is covered in a gold blanket. My mother's back is covered in blood, and I look down to see a sword on the floor near my feet.

"You did well. You are so powerful already,

though it should be me defending you, my baby girl," my mother whispers to the baby and moves the blanket covering the baby, revealing the baby's blue hair. The baby cries loudly, and my mother cries too, pressing a kiss onto the baby's head. I step back as tears stream down my face, as I know I'm watching the moment right after I used my holy fire rune to kill all these demons. I was a baby, a baby trying to defend my mother, and I failed to save her.

"Eella!" someone desperately screams, and I sharply turn to see a woman running into the room, dropping a blood-covered sword on the floor. She looks a little like my mother, only her hair is short and her face covered in blood. The woman falls on the bed, taking in my mother's injuries. "Oh sister, what have they done to you?"

"They know who she is. Take her. Hide her. It is too late for me," my mother pleads with her sister. My aunt.

"I promise," my aunt vows, harshly wiping her eyes as she picks up the baby—well, me—and holds her close to her chest as the baby cries loudly.

"Go. Just go, they are coming, and they want her dead. She cannot die, not after her father…" my mum pleads desperately, pushing at her sister's arm, but she doesn't have the strength to even move her an inch. My aunt leans over my mum, kissing her forehead and moving some of the hair out of her eyes as my mum rolls onto her back.

"Evelina will be safe. You will not have died for nothing. She will live and avenge you. I love you so much," my aunt cries out as my mum places her hand on the baby's head, on top of the blanket, leaving blood marks with her fingers.

"I only want her to be happy and alive. Nothing else even matters. I love you, my baby girl. Now live," my mother just about coughs out, and her hand falls away, her head falling to the side so her glazed-over eyes meet mine. I jump back, seeing my aunt crying in anger and running out of the room with me in her arms, but I do not look away from my mother.

"I am sorry, and I *will* avenge you. We should have been together, mum, and maybe I will see you in death one day, and we can be together. I am alive, and there were moments I was happy. Even now, I am happy to have been able to see you once again," I manage to say as I try not to break down with the anger and emotion that are trying to destroy me. I reach out to put my hand on my mother's cheek, but the tips of my fingers turn into smoke and reappear when I move my hand away.

"Guards! Call the guards!" a man shouts, and I turn to see a hooded man run into the room, lowering his cloak. It is keeper Cadean who doesn't look one bit shocked at the sight of the dead queen. Two other keepers run into the room, gasping in shock and lowering their heads in respect.

"The evil child she spawned has killed her, and her sister is protecting the baby. We must hunt the child! Now!" keeper Cadean shouts, and the two other keepers quickly run out of the room. Keeper Cadean walks over to my mother, leaning down so he is only a breath away from me as he whispers.

"You deserved this, and I will find the child and dispose of her as well. Your other children will be brought up in my care, and one will be a much better queen than you ever were."

The room spins as I scream and try to attack keeper Cadean, and suddenly there is massive white light that blinds me.

"She is coming around, any moment now," Charmeine's voice drifts over to me, the white light blinding me for only a few minutes before her face comes into view along with the whole room. I sharply sit up, looking over at Danike who is staring at the ground as he sits up.

"You…" I can't even say the words as anger fills

me, and I jump at him, lifting my hand and punching him hard in the face. He falls to the ground as I stand over him. "Where were you when my mother died?! How could you let her die like that for having your child?! Where the hell were you?!" I scream at him, and Charmeine tries to wrap an arm around me, but I push her away. I wait until he finally looks up at me before trying to speak, but no words come out. Tears stream down his face, the emotion on his face so difficult to watch, but I can't feel anything but anger. He left her alone, and me. She is dead, and he could have stopped that.

"I loved your mother and never knew she was dead. I never knew the baby, you, survived. You shouldn't have, and she shouldn't have died saving you," he spits out angrily, and I take a step back in shock. He sharply stands up, glaring at me once before storming out the house.

"He didn't mean that. You're his daughter. It is just a shock," Charmeine tries to comfort me. "He loved your mother more than his own life."

"Oh, he meant it, and I don't care. Now, how do I get out of here? I have things I need to do," I say, straightening my back and forgetting about the asshole outside. I have never needed my parents, and I'm not about to start now. But I do need revenge for many things. I think I should start making a list at this rate. My revenge list. I like the sound of it.

"We can't—" she starts off, and the door bangs open as Danike runs in.

"The souls are attacking the angels! Your sister is there!" Danike shouts at us and runs back out.

"No!" Charmeine screams in fear and runs out the door. I pause for a second, wondering if I should just leave them to it, but I know I can't do that. I shake my head before I run after them, knowing they will need all the help they can get. I guess we are going to fight some souls then... without weapons. *Awesome fucking plan.*

Chapter Six

TREX

"WHAT'S WRONG WITH HIM? Is he hurt?" Hali asks from behind me as I drop my brother onto the sofa in the lounge. He doesn't even stir, and I just rub the back of my neck as I look down at him as he starts lightly snoring. Getting as drunk as he can be is not fixing our problems. We need Nix on his game in case we are found, but getting him to listen to me is another thing altogether.

"Don't drink alcohol, kid, this is what happens," I point at Nix as I turn around to face Hali. It's clear she has been crying again, and I don't know what to do or say to her. Fuck, she lost Evie, her only family, and she is stuck with us idiots. I don't blame her for crying every day. I guess I could make her more chocolate cookies, that made her smile for a little bit. Or watch that show where they catch fake people online. She loves that too.

"I will get him a blanket, it's cold and I don't want him cold," she says, nodding to herself and running off towards the bedrooms at the back of the cabin. The girl is too nice for her own good. The dickhead deserves to be cold. I walk over to the kitchen and open the fridge, pulling out a bottle of water as I hear the front door open. I look back as Connor walks in, his cloak covered in snow and Star walking next to him. Star shakes all the snow off her back before running to me, pressing her head against my hip. The tiger has grown extremely quickly in the last month, and I think she may be some kind of magical creature. Normal tigers don't triple in size like she has in such a short time, and she is far too intelligent.

"Anything?" I ask Connor as he pulls his cloak off. Connor looks like shit, his hair is overgrown, sticking up in all directions, and he has grown a beard. We all don't know what to do with ourselves now, and we all regret everything that happened in Hell. Some of us more than others.

"The path is completely snowed in, and we can't get to town until it clears. I would burn it down with the rune or portal, but I think it will attract too much attention to us. The whole idea of living on this stupid island at the top of Scotland is to be unseen," Connor mutters, hanging his cloak on the hook next to our other ones.

"We have enough food for a week. If it becomes urgent, we will use our powers," I reply, undoing the bottle lid and drinking some of the water. I push my hair out of my eyes, knowing I need to cut it.

"Where did you find him?" Connor asks, coming over to me as Hali comes out one of the rooms with a red blanket in her arms.

"On the roof, surrounded by empty bottles of beer and god knows what else. He must have opened a portal to get them, risking us all," I growl out, shaking my head at Nix. We need to hide because not only do the witches want Hali, the Protectors want us for breaking her out and running from them. Not that any of us want anything to do with the Protectors after what Erica did. Erica would kill us in a heartbeat if we came near them anyway.

"Nix isn't taking Evie's death well, maybe we should give him a bit of a break," Connor says, which is a big understatement, and we always seem to give my brother a break when we both lose people. I thought I had some of my brother back while we were in Hell, but Evie's death has only destroyed him more. He doesn't talk to us or do anything other than drink. The only one he ever replies to is Hali, only because she threw a bucket of ice water over him for ignoring her. That kid is just like Evie because I could imagine her doing that.

"None of us are," I reply coldly, watching Hali cover up Nix with a blanket and wondering if the kid will ever be able to have a normal life without Evie protecting her. There is only so much we can do to protect her when we don't know the world of witches and demons like Evie did. Star unexpectedly starts growling low, a rumbling noise, as she runs over to Hali and Nix, pushing Hali behind her. Hali flashes me a worried look as I slide my sword off the counter, hearing Connor pick up a weapon too as he runs over to Hali. Hali stays behind Star as we stop on either side of her, listening out for anything. I pull my sleeve up my arm, getting ready to call my portal rune if we need an escape.

"What is it, girl?" I ask Star, following her gaze to the other side of the room. A wall of fire burns into existence, looking like a door for a second before Azi steps out and the fire portal burns away. Star stops growling, and I wonder for a brief second how it is even possible she knew he was coming. Azi is oddly wearing the same clothes as the last time we saw him ages ago. *Where the hell has he been?* Azi looks at us all before focusing on Hali.

"Azi!" Hali shouts, clearly happy as she slides around Star and runs at him. He picks her up in an embrace, holding her close as she bursts into tears.

"Evie…she is dead," Hali sobs out, and Azi strokes her hair as he holds her close. He lets her go and goes to his knees, so he is on her level as he is so much taller than her. Azi places his hands on her shoulders, keeping eye contact with her.

"Death is not the end. Do you remember me telling you that once? My mother and father spoke those words to me before they died, and they are very true," he says gently and leans closer, whispering something I cannot hear.

"Death is not the end," Hali replies as he pulls away, her voice filled with a little hope, and it makes me want to punch Azi. She doesn't need to be filled with false hope that Evie is somehow going to walk through the door.

"Now, I need to talk to the Protectors alone," Azi tells her firmly and she nods, wiping her eyes. He straightens up, looking over at me.

"I missed you, these guys are boring as hell!" Hali exclaims, getting all our attention.

"Cheeky shit," Connor mumbles. "I played Cluedo with you, and that game is not boring." Hali just rolls her eyes at him as Azi smiles down at her.

"Star, come on," Hali says, walking away towards the bedrooms. Star pushes her head against Azi who gives the tiger a slightly confused look as she follows after Hali.

"How did the tiger get so big? Did you buy a new one?" Azi asks curiously.

"Fuck knows. She isn't a normal tiger, that's for sure," Connor replies and shrugs his shoulders. I doubt we will ever know the answers to what Star is.

"Why are you here? We are protecting Hali, and we don't need you filling her head with ideas that Evie might come back. The kid is heartbroken enough," I snap at Azi, and he growls low as his red eyes glow.

"I am not filling her head with false promises. Evie will return. You do not understand," he growls out, and I cross my arms, raising my eyebrows at him. He can't honestly expect me to believe that bullshit. People die. They don't just come back because someone says so.

"Then tell us. We will do anything to get her

back," Connor says, his voice bordering on a little desperate, and it makes me want to punch Azi even more. Fucking hell, he is getting everyone's hopes up.

"I need you to explain exactly what happened in Hell. Do not leave a single thing out," Azi asks, but it comes out as more of a demand.

"Erica…she was behind it all," Connor answers.

"Who is Erica?" Azi asks, looking confused.

"One of the princesses we were looking for, and she is Evie's sister. We didn't know who Evie was or how messed up Erica is," Connor says, and I feel guilty that I didn't know a thing about my ex-fiancé. She was good at hiding who she really is, and that cost Evie her life. I will always regret that, and I will find a way to get my revenge for Evie. She did not deserve to be betrayed like that. I always looked up to the royal family, like everyone did, even far enough to agree to an engagement based on our strong bloodlines. Yet, everything I have learnt is making me think the royals are not people to respect at all. The only one who acted like a royal the whole time I knew her, turned out to be one. Evie carried that commanding and beautiful nature I heard her mother had. I remember the keepers once saying how Erica was nothing like her mother and so much like her father. Erica hated that they said that, and that I had accidently heard. They were right.

"Evie is a royal Protector?" Azi asks, his voice laced with confusion, and I simply nod. "What she said is true," he mutters under his breath, sounding shocked.

"What who said?" I ask.

"Nothing. You said her sister killed her?" he enquires.

"Erica set it all up to get Evie off guard. She knew she couldn't just kill Evie on her own with no plan," Connor explains. We all know Erica couldn't have beat Evie one to one. Evie grew up on the streets, and she was a fantastic fighter, not that I ever told her that. Erica was taught to fight by old Protectors who had never had a real fight in their lives and we were lucky to have a mentor who fought in the angel war. Protectors only ever had to fight demons who could be killed with one run and no fight needed. Evie fought everything, and that made her strong.

"My brothers helped her," Azi muses. "They were the only way Erica could have gotten into that layer."

"Yes," I sharply reply, and he seems lost in thought for a while, looking down at his arms even though you can't see anything with his suit on.

"Where is Evie's body? I need to see her," Azi eventually says, lifting his gaze to us.

"She disappeared," I reply, remembering the moment Evie's eyes glazed over and her body disappeared into nothing but white dust. That memory haunts me, keeps me up at night. Much like the thoughts of her impossibly deep blue eyes that understood me without a word leaving her lips.

"What? No...that isn't possible," Azi says, shaking his head as he starts to pace. "She can't have disappeared. Her soul would have left her body and that was it."

"Her soul never left. She didn't die like anything else I've ever seen," I honestly answer. Demons turn into piles of blue or sometimes black dust, but their soul always leaves their body, and you see the light leave them. Evie's death has haunted me for far too long because I can't understand where her soul went, and there is no one to ask for answers.

"Because she didn't die. Her father must have been an angel...I know where she is!" Azi shockingly exclaims and grins. "I knew death could not take my Evie so easily."

"Where is she? I can answer that, she is dead. Angel or not, you cannot survive being stabbed three times!" I shout at him.

"No, she isn't dead, and you need to trust me on that. I have lived far too long and seen things you would not believe, Protector. Angels are complicated, and I know Evie is half angel," Azi says, and hope fills me as I step forward.

"Find her and bring her back. We need her," I say, not wanting to admit how much I need to see her just one more time. I need…well, I need to protect her. I owe her a debt, and I miss her. Even the snarky, annoying attitude she has. My eyes lock with Azi's as he nods, a small smirk on his lips.

"Oh, I am going to find my Evie and bring her back, so she can get her revenge. Erica will regret killing her sister in such a cowardly way. No coward is going to be queen of the Protectors or anything," Azi states firmly, and I agree.

"And we will be at her side. We will be her Protectors," Connor states, bowing his head a little. "She deserves to be queen. She deserves revenge, which we can help her get."

"Find her," I say simply, as Azi calls a portal. He nods once at me before stepping into it and disappearing. I walk towards the door, pulling it open.

"Where are you going?" Connor asks.

"To get a bucket of snow to wake my brother up. We need to be ready. Our princess is coming back, and she is bringing one hell of a fight with her."

Chapter Seven

EVIE

"SHIT-A-DOODLE," I mutter, seeing the fifty-some-odd souls banging the door and walls of an old building in the middle of a few small ones. I would guess it is a church, but I'm not too sure. The roof is covered in souls too, making it impossible for the angels trapped inside to even fly out. The walls are cracking under the pressure, and the souls are pulling tiles off the roof to get inside. I can hear a few of the angels screaming in the building, and we have to hope they aren't being killed already. The logical side of me wants to run away, but it isn't the right thing to do. I won't ever be the one that runs from something difficult. I look over at my father, not knowing what to make of him. I know that I'm half wanting to pick him up and drop him in the souls for being an asshole. I smile a little at the bruise on his face, at least I have that.

"They are all inside, and we need to get them out," Danike points out the obvious as we hide in a large alley between two white houses.

"We need a distraction," I muse, searching around for one and seeing nothing. Okay, so we need to be the distraction. Danike and Charmeine look back at me with a questioning look.

"Any ideas?" Charmeine asks.

"So, you can boost powers, right? Like maybe my holy fire rune for example?" I ask, knowing my idea is a little crazy, but usually the crazy ideas are the only ones that work. She nods, looking a little confused.

"Possibly. I mean you aren't full angel, so I don't know how it would work boosting your powers. You cannot fight all these on your own. Nobody could do that," she says and sighs. "I want to save them, but not lose you for it."

"One, I have no plan on dying again any time soon," I tell her, "and two, I was thinking we get their attention and run them back to this alley. We can make a wall of fire to escape as Danike gets the angels out," I say.

"What if a soul catches you?" Danike says.

"Acting like the caring father now? No thanks," I snap, and he shakes his head as he looks away. "I'm also a good fighter, so I can kick some of the souls away or hit them with something if they get too close to us," I do explain to them both, only because Charmeine looks worried. I look around, only seeing a few fallen branches as anything I could use to defend myself. I might be able to find a stone though. At least it is something.

"That's crazy. They could catch us, or the boost could fail. I've never worked with a half angel before. Most die—" Charmeine goes to say.

"Enough," Danike growls, and Charmeine looks away with red cheeks. *What was that about?* I look back as the souls start climbing the walls of the building, going for the windows by the looks of it.

"We do this, or they all die. I don't think we have any other choice," I state, knowing we don't have time to argue between ourselves. Danike and Charmeine look between each other, and then back to me.

"Let's do this," Danike says firmly, though he doesn't look happy about it. His wings spread out behind him before he shoots up into the sky.

"We need to distract them all and make a lot of noise," I warn Charmeine of my plan, before running out of the houses and straight towards the building nearest to the souls. They don't notice us as we get closer, and I grab a shiny, sharp stone off the ground to defend myself with. I put my back against the wall of the house and wait for Charmeine to do the same.

"On the count of three, we both run out and scream—as loud as you can—and then we run towards the alley. Keep screaming, and I will run behind you, keeping an eye out," I tell her.

"Screaming and running, that I can do perfectly," she jokes nervously, making me smile a little.

"One...two...three," I count, and we run out, catching a few souls' attention by doing that alone. We scream and scream, seeing all the souls slowly turn to us. The ones on the roof jump down, and the ones on the walls slide down them. This close, the souls are disgusting, far worse than the usual ones on the first layer. These are dripping with a black liquid, parts of their faces and skin falling off, and most of them don't even have eyes. They all suddenly run at us, tripping over each other to get to us first. We run as fast as we can towards the alley between the houses, with Charmeine just in front of me. Charmeine suddenly trips on a broken branch, falling over face first into the grass. *Shit.* I spin around in front of her, leaning down to pick the branch up and swinging it at the first soul that gets me.

"Fly!" Charmeine screams behind me, and I call my wings. I'm too late as dozens of souls run at me as my feet leave the ground. One of them grabs my foot, pulling me down into them as I desperately try to fly away.

"Evie!" I hear my name screamed by a familiar voice as the souls pull me down, and then there is fire everywhere just as everything goes black and my head slams on the ground.

Chapter Eight

AZI

THE PORTAL BURNS INTO EXISTENCE, the pressure of going to the one place I knew was impossible to ever travel to without a great cost burning through my thoughts. The cost doesn't flash through my mind, not even for a second, as I make the portal larger and feel the massive drain on my power. I growl low as sweat drips down my head, and finally, the portal breaks the barrier to a place I never thought I would go to. I jump through the portal, landing on top of a white brick house as I take in everything. A screaming angel draws my attention behind me where a white-haired angel is running away from an army of souls, screaming her head off. My heart catches in my throat as Evie runs around a wall, a stone in her hand as the army of souls is just behind her. *What the hell is she doing?* The blonde angel trips, falling flat on her face in the grass. Evie picks up a fallen branch, spinning around and swinging it at a soul as I jump off the house and start running towards her. I run around a house just in time to see small black wings appear on her back, and she flies into the air, only to be caught around the foot by a soul. The souls slowly pull her down as I run, jumping over walls to get to her in time.

"Evie!" I shout as more souls get hold of her, and I call my fire into my hands. I run and jump right into the middle of the souls where Evie disappeared, praying that she will survive this. *I can't exist without her.* I send out streams of fire as I kneel over Evie as she lies on the floor. The souls scream as I increase the fire until every single one of them is gone and there is complete, deadly silence. I step off her, pushing her shiny blue hair out of her face and feeling for a pulse on her neck. I glance at her body, seeing three bites on her lower legs and one on her shoulder.

"Evie! No!" the white-haired angel screams, running over to us, and kneeling on her other side.

"Heal her! Now!" I growl at the angel, who jumps back when she sees my face.

"I-I can't alone. It isn't my gift, but it is my sister's," she rushes out.

"Get her then. If Evie dies, I will kill everyone here!" I shout, and she quickly runs off when she sees how serious I am. Two souls run out from behind a house at the angel, and I know they will kill her before she can get help if I don't help her. I jump up, shooting fire balls at them as the angel takes off into the sky, and they burn away.

"Azi?" Evie gasps out, and I fall back down to my knees, picking her up and holding her to my chest. Her blue eyes gaze up at me, her soft black wings move slightly under my hands. I just stare at her beautiful features, her high cheekbones, her soft pink lips. Everything about her is perfect to me.

"I thought I lost you," I whisper, and she chuckles, her face contorting in pain with the movements. I glance at the bite on her shoulder, seeing the poison from the bite crawling up her arm. They need to heal her before the poison hits her heart.

"Don't go being sloppy on me now. Where has the big, bad demon gone?" she replies.

"He fell for a girl who regularly likes to give him

a heart attack, that's where," I say with a low chuckle, making her smile even though she hides the pain she is in. I can see it in her eyes, in her shallow breaths.

"You should have picked better then," she replies.

"I picked the best, and I wouldn't change you for the world. When you are better, I'm going to show you how much you mean to me and never let you out my sight, Vi," I tell her firmly. Her eyes flutter a little before they close, and her skin feels freezing cold under my hands. I look around, knowing we don't have time and I can't portal her out of here while she is like this. It could kill her.

"Lay her down," the angel shouts, landing in front of us with another angel. This one is clearly younger, and very clearly her sister with their similar features. This girl has her long, white hair up in a ponytail, a ripped dress covered in black dust and blood on her. As I lay Evie down carefully, I spot another angel crouched on a wall near us, watching our every move. His eyes are mainly locked on Evie, and he looks familiar which is impossible. His eyes meet mine, and he suddenly looks away.

"Ignore Danike," the blonde angel suggests, catching my attention. "Heal her, Scarlett!"

"I'm not good with my powers. They won't work, Charmeine," Scarlett nervously says, looking between Evie and me.

"You can do this. I believe in you," Charmeine tells her, grabbing her hands and placing them on Evie's stomach. Evie's head rolls to the side as she goes completely unconscious, and I frantically look at Charmeine.

"Heal her or she will die!" I shout at them both desperately. Charmeine places her hands on her sister's head, a white glow coming from them. Scarlett's hands start glowing a little on Evie's stomach, but I know it's not enough.

"More! Push everything you can into healing her! She is our family, heal her!" Charmeine shouts, and Scarlett screams as a white light blasts out of her hands, sending me flying backwards into the side of building. I smack against the wall, cracking it in places, and brick falls down onto me. I have to hold my hands in front of my face from the light as I try to stand up. The light suddenly disappears, and I run over, dropping to my knees next to Evie and Scarlett as they lie next to each other passed out. I pull Evie to me, seeing the bites are gone and a little colour in her pale cheeks.

"You're going to be okay," I whisper to her, and kiss her forehead. *I'm not letting anything happen to my Evie again.*

Chapter Nine

EVIE

"WHO THE FUCK do you think you are to tell me what to do, angel?" Azi growls, his chest vibrating with anger as my head is pressed tightly against it. His smoky and somewhat sweetly seductive scent comforts me for only a second as I realise it's really Azi. *How is he here?* Azi is no angel. Unless the angels lied to me, which I highly doubt.

"Am I dead?" I ask, pulling away and looking up at Azi who holds me in his arms. He lets me down as I wriggle and sway on my feet.

"No, Vi, I wouldn't let you die," Azi tells me firmly, holding his hand on my shoulder. I blink my eyes into focus, seeing Danike standing in front of us, his arms crossed as he stares down Azi. *Bad move.* I look around him to see Charmeine hugging a girl who I assume is her sister by the looks of it. Right behind them is a crowd of angels, all of them looking at us expectantly.

"What do you want?" I ask Danike.

"We need your demon to open a portal, so we can all leave and return to earth," Danike answers. He doesn't even give a shit about me, he only cares about escaping here. Go figure.

"I am taking Evie, and that is it. This place was made to keep you away from humans and demons," Azi says, and Danike narrows his eyes.

"I knew most demons were selfish bastards, but you are willing to let us all die?" Danike exclaims.

"Azi, can we talk alone?" I ask, not wanting him to answer that, and he looks down at me before nodding.

"Don't be long. The souls will come back," Danike warns us as we start to turn away.

"We will be as long as we want. You don't get to tell me what I can and can't do," I warn Danike, who looks close to losing his shit until Charmeine places her hand on his arm and he walks away. I walk straight to the far house I see in the distance, with Azi keeping himself close to my side.

"Who is he to you?" Azi asks. "And can I kill him? I find him annoying."

"My father, and trust me, if anyone has a reason to kill him, it's me," I reply. Azi places his hand on my back, comforting me without any words.

"Angel...I didn't expect that," Azi finally says into the silence.

"Neither did I. The wings are strange," I say, and I see Azi looking at them.

"They are stunning and suit you," he replies. *Smooth, real smooth.*

"I wouldn't go that far," I chuckle in return, nudging his shoulder. Azi opens the door to the house, letting me go in before coming in himself and shutting it.

"Hali? You did get her? Or we need to leave right now?" I say the moment the door is shut. I couldn't say anything in front of the angels, I don't need them knowing about Hali when I cannot trust them all. Azi steps into my space, placing his hands on the top of my arms.

"The Protectors broke Hali out and have hidden with her. I saw Hali before I came here, and she is heartbroken but perfectly okay," he says, and I sigh in relief until I process what he just said. *The Protectors did what?*

"They did what?" I ask in disbelief.

"Saved Hali. It seems you have their respect, even when they think you're dead," he tells me.

"I will have to thank them. I owe them now," I mutter. I'd rather owe Azi, and he is a demon. I don't have a clue how I could pay back the Protectors for such a debt.

"You act so much like a demon with your need to repay favours," Azi mutters.

"I was mainly brought up around them, and I find their way of life to be right," I answer and then think of something. "How did you get here? The angels say they can't escape."

"They can't, and only an overlord can get in— and out—of here. My father made this place, and we were all told that coming here would cost all the worlds a great price," he explains, his words spoken low, and I can sense he feels some shame in breaking a no doubt important promise to his father. I don't know much about his parents, only that Azi respected and loved them. To break anything he promised them, well it means a fucking lot.

"Still you came for me?" I whisper.

"Evie, fuck. Don't you know by now that I will follow you anywhere? Even if you don't want me there and hate me…my place is at your side," he says, sliding his hands up my shoulders and to my neck. I don't move as his one hand slides to the back of my neck, and he pulls my lips to his. His hands rest on my neck as he passionately kisses me, the way I remember his kisses being. Perfect. Incredible and so seductive that you forget the entire world around you. I fist my hands in his hair as he picks me up by my ass, turning us around and lying me down on the table.

"We shouldn't. We have a lot to do and—" I stop as Azi lifts my leg, kissing the inside of my leg, my voice catching in my throat.

"There is nothing we can't leave until later," he tells me, kissing my thigh this time as he steps into the space between my legs. I lean up on my elbows as Azi goes to push my dress up and flashes me a wicked grin.

"We have a problem!" Charmeine shouts, and then bangs on the door. "The souls are back, and we need to leave!"

"For fuck's sake," Azi groans, and I feel exactly the same. I slide off the table, pulling the door open and knowing I need to find some time alone with Azi to repeat this again.

Chapter Ten

"WHERE ARE THEY?" I ask Charmeine at the door, stepping out where all the angels are gathered together. She points in the distance, where there is a massive crowd of souls running for us. We still have a few minutes, but not a lot.

"Azi?" I ask, and he gently grabs my arm, pulling me away from Charmeine.

"We don't know all these angels, and if we take them, they could attack everyone. Earth was nearly lost once because of an angel attack," he explains in a whisper so no one else hears. If everyone blamed entire races for the actions of a few, no one would be left alive. I won't think like that. I look over at the group of angels, most of them are sitting on the floor and giving up. Others are stood proudly, watching us for our answer. Danike, Charmeine and her sister are talking quietly, Danike's eyes drifting to me every few seconds.

"And if we leave them, that's on us. It would be genocide because of something they didn't do," I harshly whisper back.

"It won't be genocide. You will be coming back," he says.

"Not without them I won't," I tell him, crossing my arms and stepping one step back towards the angels.

"Don't be stubborn now," he mutters, rubbing his face.

"I'm not. I'm being normal and doing the right thing," I tell him, not keeping my voice down, and I hear the angels whispering behind me.

"God, I hate your moral compass at times. Fine," he says, stepping around me and walking to stand in front of the angels.

"You like me really, demon," I tease, moving to stand at his side and chuckling at the glare he gives me before addressing the angels.

"I will open a portal to earth, which you will need to run through as quickly as possible. Do not be alarmed if you pass out, demon and angel magic don't mix well," Azi shouts. I glance behind us, seeing the horde of souls getting that much closer. The angels all cheer, looking between each other, and a few hug. I spot five who stand slightly away from the others, they are all men and have cold looks on their faces.

"I give you one warning though," I shout, and everything goes silent. "If you cause any problems, any danger to earth, or kill anyone without reason…I will come after you. You do not want that."

"And she will not be alone," Azi says as I keep my eyes locked on the five angels. The one in the middle lowers his head and nods in agreement. That's all I need, and I will have to trust them for now.

"Time to go! I need my sword and a bacon sandwich, asap," I say, holding my hands on my hips.

"Trust you to bring up bacon at a time like this," he says, chuckling as he holds his hands out.

"No time is bad for bacon," I shake my head at him, believing he should know that by now, and then step away as he calls the portal. The portal burns into existence, bigger than the usual one he does for one person. I glance at Azi, seeing red veins covering his face from his burning red eyes.

His demon is close to taking over with all this power, and we don't need that to happen here.

"Run in the portal or stay! Now!" I shout at the angels who stare in shock. They quickly move, running through the portal two at a time. Charmeine grabs her sister's hand, nodding once at me before jumping into the portal. Danike stands, waiting by the portal until every angel is gone but Azi and me, before jumping himself. I walk towards the portal, standing right in front of it as it burns, and the heat hurts my skin a little.

"Go," Azi bites out when I look back, seeing how much he is struggling. I quickly jump into the portal, the fire feeling like it burns away my soul before darkness thankfully takes over.

Chapter Eleven

EVIE

I ROLL ONTO MY BACK, groaning as every part
of me hurts, and I force my eyes open to see where
Azi has portalled to. I'm surprised to find us all
outside his manor house on the outskirts of
London, which thankfully has high walls, so no one
can see in. I pull myself up, looking around at all
the angels still unconscious on the floor and spin
around just as Azi falls through the portal, landing
roughly on his knees. I rush to him, jumping over
two angels and sliding down in front of him. I lift
his head, seeing his red eyes are glowing, and there
are veins crawling all over his face, but his demon
hasn't taken over. I relax a little when he smirks at
me, the lines disappear, and I push some of his

black hair off his damp forehead. It took way too much of him to save the angels and me.

"That was dangerous, if I wasn't in control," he quietly tells me, while he is still struggling to catch his breath.

"You are always in control, Azi. I know that," I whisper to him.

"I could have not been in control, and that is really dangerous for someone like me. I'm a demon, and you should know that when my inner demon takes over, he doesn't recognise people. Especially not people I am in love with and would never usually hurt," he whispers the words quietly and so full of emotion that I find it hard to look away.

"Azi, I'm not scared of you, and you shouldn't be scared of who you are," I tell him, needing him to understand that. What I don't tell him is that if his demon took over, I would be running my ass away as quickly as possible.

I stand and turn around, looking at all the angels plastered across the lawn of Azi's gardens. They all look okay, nothing particularly wrong with them that I can see anyways. I think for a second about the fact I could have made a big mistake and these angels could be evil, but I know I can figure out a way to kill them if they betray us. I am glad that Azi decided to bring us here. It is probably the best place for these angels, hidden from the world until we figure something out, and they can get to understand everything that has no doubt changed since they were last here. I look up at the giant house, which I've only been to a few times, and admire how good it feels to see something of colour again. My eyes drift to a purple flower crawling up the side of the house, reminding me of Hali as it's her favourite colour. We need to leave soon to find Hali and let her know I am alive. I can't even imagine how upset she must have been. A tiny part of me wants to go and see the Protectors, but I don't think on that for long. They might not want to see me, knowing who I am and who I am going to kill to get my revenge. I won't let anyone stop me, no matter what they say or do.

"They will not wake up for a while. Should we go inside?" I ask, though I don't see the point in waiting for a reply. I don't wait for his answer as I step over the angels and walk straight towards the house. Azi's house is looking extremely beautiful and old. I look at the old stone building, the beautiful brown brick walls and the white windows. There are rose bushes planted outside, and they are loads of different colours which look extremely beautiful. I open the white door, looking round at the small entrance hall, which is covered in white sheets, and the grand staircase that goes up to the second floor. I briefly try to remember where kitchens are in this house, and I turn to the right to have a look on that side. I find the kitchen straight-away, and I head straight for the fridge, opening it up and seeing the zero food inside.

"Why can't I find any bacon? It feels like it's been years since I've had anything decent to eat that isn't a bloody white vegetable," I mutter and slam the fridge door shut. I turn around to see Azi leaning against the door, a smirk permanently etched across his face.

"I could go to *Greggs* to get you a bacon sand-wich," he suggests. I lean against the fridge as a big smile takes over my face.

"And what would I have to do to make you go get it for me?" I ask. Azi just smiles and walks straight out of the door to no doubt make a portal outside so it doesn't burn his wood floors.

"I didn't ask anything, I know if you don't have bacon for a while, you get really moody. It's likely safer for everybody if I go and get you some while we wait for the angels to wake up," he chuckles before he leaves. He has a point. I smile and find a bottle of water in one of the cupboards before walking back outside and sitting on a wall as I wait for the angels to wake up. The angels don't stir for some time while I drink my water. As I watch them, I wonder how angry the world might be to know there are angels around again. I look at my back, even though my wings aren't out, and wonder if having my angel wings means I will get any powers with it. I'm not sure if I want any, but with a big battle coming up, any bonus would be useful. I finally see one of the angels moving at the back. I slide off the wall and walk over to see that it is Danike that has woken up first. *Typical.*

"That portal hurt more than I remember them ever hurting," he comments as he stands up and then pauses as he looks around where we are. I silently watch his reaction to being outside of hell for the first time in twenty-six years. I do not know what it must feel like to him, but I imagine it's good to see a colour other than white. The other angels all start stirring, some of them climbing up off the ground and looking around in shock. I watch as Charmeine stirs and rolls on her side. She places her hand on her sister's arm, right next to her, before realising that she is still sleeping. She stretches her hand out in the grass and picks up a small daisy, staring at it in amazement. Her eyes meet mine as she stands up and walks over to me.

"Thank you for taking us out of there. We could never have escaped without your help, and we will always owe you our lives," she says and presses the daisy into my hand as a gift.

"You do not have to thank me. You owe me nothing," I reply, accepting the flower. She only shakes her head at me before walking away to wait for her sister to wake up most likely.

"The angels will come if you need them," Danike says from next to me. I look at the man who is my father and feel nothing but anger towards him. He left my mother alone when he must have known the cost of doing that. He left me alone and has had no interest in even being decent towards me since he found out he is my father. I know that I do not need a father like that in my life.

"I will never call for the angels. I have survived on my own since I was a baby, and it has taught me that I do not need anyone in my life, especially not a father who left a pregnant woman alone," I say harshly, "who left a defenseless child alone."

"I did not leave her alone, and you have no idea what you speak. You will need the angels, especially if you plan to take the throne. The keepers will never accept a half angel like you as their queen," he warns me.

"It is lucky that Evie has more people to protect her than you know. The keepers will have no choice in the matter if it is what Evie wants," Azi's dark voice comes from right behind me.

"Demons cannot protect angels from the price we all pay," he tells Azi and then looks towards me. "When you want to know about who you are and the price you will pay, come to me."

"There is no price that I cannot pay. I have everything I need, without your help," I tell him as Azi slides an arm around my waist.

"You and your people can stay in my home for as long as you wish. We have to leave, but there are humans who will come to the house to bring food and clothes once a week. I suggest you all get to know the world you have stepped into before going out in it," Azi says, and Danike nods his agreement.

"Good luck," Danike says once, his eyes locked on mine before he walks away. I try not to feel any emotion that the only parent I've known just walks away like I do not mean anything to him. Thankfully Azi uses that moment to show me the bacon sandwich, which I practically inhale in two seconds, and it makes me feel so much better. I smile up at

Azi, knowing how lucky I am to have him in my life and how much I missed him. I don't know when it was, the saving my life or getting me bacon, but I can't help but feel like we are getting back to how we were before. Once I'm done eating, I look up at Azi with only one question in mind.

"Where is Hali?"

Chapter Twelve

ONCE AZI TELLS me where to find Hali, I open a portal with my rune and run through it, feeling the cold wash of the magic surrounding me as I step into an empty room. The room is small with a kitchen pressed on one side of it, and the lounge with two sofas on the other side. There is a red blanket hanging over the back of the sofa and weapons all leaning up against it. I hear Azi come through the portal after me, and I turn and give him a questioning look.

"Hali!" Azi shouts. I practically hold my breath as a door opens and Hali steps out, dropping the book she was holding. Hali's long black hair is neatly braided, and she has on black clothes I've never seen her wear before. They almost look like boy clothes, and I wonder if the Protectors went shopping for her or something. Neither one of us moves for a second, then she runs into my arms, crying and mumbling words I can't understand. I hold her close to me, rubbing my hand down her back in comfort as I try not to cry myself. I missed her, and damn, I hate that she had to go through all this heartbreak and shock. She has been through enough.

"I'm okay, honestly," I tell her, but I know that she probably won't believe me, and she pulls away to look me in the eye.

"They told me you had died, and I don't really understand how you're back," she mumbles, wiping her eyes.

"It's a little complicated, and you would probably laugh if I told you," I say, and she gives me a confused look. I step back and call on my wings, watching Hali's very shocked reaction as she stares at me. Hali walks to my side and gently touches the wings.

"You are an angel?" she asks.

"I didn't think I'd ever say yes to the question before," I reply and go to explain more when the door bangs open behind us. I turn just in time to see a gigantic tiger jump on top of me, knocking me to the floor. I am just about to defend myself when the tiger licks my face, and I realise who it is. Star is huge, her head is the size of a small child and she weighs a tonne. I push her head away to get her to stop licking my cheek. So gross.

"Star?" I ask in shock, because this is not the baby tiger I feel like I only left a while ago. Star climbs off me but still stays close as I manage to pull myself up.

"Evie?" a shocked voice asks as I place a hand on Star's head. I look towards the door, seeing Connor and Trex stood there like statues. They both have snow-covered cloaks on and look so different from when I last saw them. Connor's hair has grown out, and he now has a beard which really suits him. When his gold eyes meet mine, I can do nothing but stare for a moment as the tension flitters between us.

"Blue?" Connor asks, his voice like someone who's just seen a ghost. Which I kinda am.

"Hey, Connor," I reply, wondering why I can't stop smiling at seeing him. I missed him, which is crazy when we didn't have that long together. He falls to his one knee, bowing his head, and I don't understand why he would do that. I look at Trex, who slowly does the same thing but keeps his dark green eyes locked on mine.

"We made a mistake, and you died because of it. If you give us another chance, we will protect you because you are a royal and we owe you," he says and lowers his head, bowing like Connor.

"Will you idiots get up off the floor? We have stuff to do, and if you really want to say sorry for letting me try and rescue my crazy-ass sister, a plate full of bacon will do nicely," I say, making everyone chuckle and killing the tension in the room.

"I saved a load of bacon in the fridge for you," Connor says standing up and coming over. He pulls me into a tight hug, and his lips graze the top of my ear. "I'm so fucking happy you're here." His words are a whisper, but so full of emotion that it gives me goose bumps.

"Can I help you cook?" Hali asks as Connor pulls away, and he grins at her.

"Sure, kid," he replies, knocking his head to the side. Hali smiles at me once before running after him to the kitchen. Trex walks over to me but goes around me to the sofa as I watch him. He moves the red blanket away, revealing my purple sword.

"You have it!" I say happily, walking over as Trex hands me it.

"Even when we thought you were dead, I wasn't letting anyone touch what is yours."

"Is that why you went after Hali?"

"No. I did that for you," he tells me, his fingers grazing mine on the sword. I give him a slightly confused look, because I swear this man hated me not so long ago.

"Where is the other one?" Azi asks, breaking up the tense moment.

"We don't know, and we were just looking for him," Trex explains.

"Why would Nix leave?" I ask.

"He is likely drunk somewhere. When we told him you were coming back, he didn't believe us and stormed out of here," Trex tells me, not looking happy about it.

"I will go and find him. Evie needs us all if she is going to do what I think she is," Azi says. I mouth 'thank you' to him, knowing I don't need to say much more as he calls a portal and disappears, leaving only burn marks on the floor.

"What do you plan to do?" Trex asks.

"Kill Erica and take the throne. What else?"

Chapter Thirteen

"SHIT, I thought you were a wall and you appeared out of fucking nowhere," I mutter, staring at the back of the huge blue demon I have just bumped into and smashed my drink against. The beer drips down his back as he turns, looking down at me like I'm a bug or something he wants squished under his giant feet. I don't have a clue what kind of demon he is, but by the sound of the humans running out of the bar, screaming at his growl, it isn't good.

"You are going to pay for that, stupid, drunk human," the demon growls and grabs me by the front of my shirt, lifting me in the air as I laugh.

"You know, it's been a boring day. Thank fuck I can finally have some fun," I manage to laugh out, and the demon's blue eyes glow as he lifts a beefy hand, slamming it into my face and sending me flying across the bar. I smash into a water fountain, wheezing from the force of that hit as I open my eyes to see everything is blurry. When things come into focus, the blue demon is reaching for me in the fountain, so I call my fire rune, making a shield of fire in front of my hand. I slam the shield into his hand, and he screams, stepping back as his hand burns. I know it was a cheap shot to use my powers, but I don't really care.

"Protector," the demon spits out as I stand up in the fountain, water dripping off my clothes, and my phone most likely destroyed in my pocket.

"Yeah, that's me," I sigh, holding my other hand out and calling a ball of fire this time.

"I'm leaving," the demon shakily gets out, and I swear under my breath as he runs away. That ruins all the fun.

"If you want someone on your playing field to take your shit out on, I'm right here, Protector," Azi drawls, walking around the fountain and pausing, picking up a bottle of whiskey that someone must have left. He opens the lid before taking a long drink.

"Pass it here," I tell the asshole as I make the holy fire disappear and jump out of the fountain, ignoring my dripping wet clothes as I walk to Azi. He passes me the whiskey and pulls out a chair, sitting down and waiting as I drink. He waves a hand at another seat and raises an eyebrow.

"You can sit your ass in it, or I can make you. Your choice," he says, his voice impassive, but I know he means what he says. Fuck's sake. I turn the chair around to face him before sitting in it and slamming the whiskey on the table between us. I know what the idiot is going to say, and I don't believe him. People don't just come back from the dead. I've spent enough time praying and pleading that my sister and mother would come back. But dead people don't just pop up alive. I have no fucking clue how he convinced my brother and Connor that Evie is alive, but I won't believe it.

"Evie is back and wants you with her. Not this drunk, lost-in-misery you, though. No, she needs the Nix who fought by her side in Hell. The Nix that makes her laugh and isn't a complete tosser most of the time," Azi tells me, then picks up the whiskey and takes a deep drink.

"You expect me to believe that shit?"

"Yes," he answers as I lean back in my chair, watching him.

"If Evie was really back, you wouldn't come to

get me for her. She liked me, and I fucking liked her, which means I'm a threat to your chances of getting her back." His eyes glow a darker red, the only reaction he has to my words.

"You're right, but I know Evie needs you. She is going to go after her sister and take the throne. She will be the queen of a race that has hunted her, that are scared of her. Every day she will be at risk," he informs me and slides the bottle across the table. I catch it before it falls off and take a long drink as I think over his words.

"None of this matters anyway, she is dead," I shake my head, throwing the bottle across the room and standing up. I'm not sitting here listening to this bullshit any longer.

"Portal to the house and see for yourself," he says, and I chuckle.

"I'm going to find another bar," I laugh, calling a portal. I'm about to walk through it when Azi grabs me by the back of my jacket and throws me in the air. I see the fire portal seconds before I go flying through it and everything goes black. When I finally open my eyes and shake my head, I sit up and look around for that fucker Azi.

"Nix?" Evie's soft yet somehow strong voice calls from behind me. I stand up, knowing I'm not sure if I can turn around and see if she is real. Maybe I died in that portal and I'm with her?

"Nix? Look at me," Evie gently commands, and then a warm hand lightly rests on my arm. I look at the hand and turn slightly, my eyes widening when I see Evie standing next to me. She looks just like I remember her, if not even more stunning. When I see the black wings on her back, I nearly step backwards, but instead I reach a hand out to them. Her eyes close as I stroke a hand down her right wing, loving how soft the feathers feel.

"Evie?" I whisper, placing my hand on her cheek. "How?"

"It's a long story," she says with a light chuckle.

"I'm sorry I failed you. I'm so sorry," I whisper, and she shakes her head, stepping closer and putting both her hands on my cheeks to make me look down into her crystal blue eyes.

"You did not fail me, you couldn't have known. Now I'm back, and I want my revenge. Will you be at my side?" she asks, and there is silence between us as I remove her hands from my face and step back. She looks heartbroken, misinterpreting my move until I go down on one knee and bow my head.

"Yes. I will fight for you. I will protect you. You

have my respect and my life, Evie," I say, and I look up when I see her hand outstretched for me. I slide my hand into hers and get up off the floor.

"No one in this room needs to bow for me. I'm a thief, assassin, and the very last thing I am is a damn princess. Now have a shower, and we can tune you in to our plan," she says, holding her hands on her hips, and I nod.

"She means the bat-shit crazy plan that is going to get us all killed," Trex mutters as he walks to my side and pats my shoulder.

"You know the craziest plans usually work out the best. Or not. Who knows?" Evie says with a shrug. She walks away from us both towards Hali, Connor and Azi in the kitchen. I missed my crazy girl.

"It's good to have you back, brother," Trex says, and pats my back a few times before following Evie. I look over at everyone in the kitchen and know this is the family I've always wanted. I finally have a chance to save someone, rather than watch them die. *I finally have a chance at a life.*

Chapter Fourteen

EVIE

"WHAT IS THE PLAN THEN?" Nix asks as he sits down next to me on the sofa, freshly showered and shaved. His long black hair is pushed out of his face, so I can see his light green eyes more clearly. He still looks and feels tired, with massive bags under his eyes, but I know he won't rest until we tell him the whole plan. We haven't actually discussed all the plan yet because Trex keeps saying it's "crazy".

"I kill Erica and take the throne. Nice and simple," I reply and Trex groans. I glance over at Hali, who is playing on an iPad and lying on top of Star in the corner. She won't leave my sight for a while, but she doesn't need to be involved in this kind of conversation.

"Nothing about that is simple. You can't just take the throne," Trex replies as Nix slides his hand into mine, linking our fingers. I don't pull away from him, which even surprises me. I kinda like his hand in mine, and I know he needs to be close.

"But I can kill Erica?" I ask. Trex looks towards Connor, who sighs and leans forward off the sofa to keep eye contact with me.

"So basically, I trained for a bit to be a keeper. I decided it wasn't for me, but I know some things that most Protectors don't. Like the fact a keeper has to acknowledge your birth as a royal before you can claim the throne."

"So, we kidnap a keeper? I don't see a problem," I say, raising an eyebrow, daring them to tell me no. I like kidnapping, it can be super fun. Though I don't tell them that, I have a feeling they won't agree. It's okay, I can train them. I catch Azi's eye, and I know he is remembering that one time we kidnapped a powerful demon that was killing other demons and draining their magic for fun. We had to take him to another demon who wanted revenge, and we got paid very well for it. It was a fun day. Like a couple's day or something that humans do.

"Keepers are powerful, extremely so. The only

person who can beat them is the queen or king. Or their knights. You get a power boost when you are chosen. The keepers are given extra power when they are chosen," Connor explains, and I lean back, thinking it over. What the hell are knights? I choose to address the bigger problem first.

"I bet I could still catch one of them," I muse, and the guys give me a worried look. "I'm good at hunting Protectors, remember? Now let's say we have a keeper and he acknowledges me, can I then kill Erica and take the throne?"

"You have a one-track mind, Vi," Azi points out with a long sigh from the other end of the sofa where he is seated on the arm. "Can't we all find a beach and live out a nice life? Fuck other people."

"Nope. That bitch stabbed me, not once, but three times. I am going to make her pay for it," I warn, my voice threatening enough to cause an awkward silence.

"Well if that is how it has to be, then we move onto the next problem…" Connor says and looks uncomfortable.

"Connor means the problem that all the Protectors are fucking batshit scared of you," Trex points out. I remember how the Protectors ran away into the elevator when they saw me the last time I was there, or the ones that fell on the floor when I said 'boo'. Oh yeah, I forgot about that.

"How do I change that?" I ask, because making friends isn't a thing I'm good at. I really have no idea why these fuckers seem to like me.

"I have an idea. Rather than just killing Erica, you go against her in the test for the throne in a month?"

"Wait, she isn't queen yet? What test?" I ask, totally confused.

"The test she killed your other sisters for, to make sure they couldn't enter," Nix says gently, carefully almost because he hates to say it out loud. I didn't know my sisters, but it hurts in my chest when he mentions them and how they died for something so pathetic.

"Explain it?" I ask, clearing my throat.

"There is a test that is offered to all heirs to the throne. It is done over three days, and no one but keepers and royals knows what goes on in it. It can only be done when the power is gathered up or it drains away. The test couldn't happen last time the power was gathered, therefore she can't be queen yet and will be waiting. The test itself is a secret, one your mother should have told you," Trex explains, and I ignore the sharp, raw pain I still feel over knowing who my mother is and how she died. Keeper Cadean's face flashes into my mind, and I tighten my grip on Nix's hand in anger. Nix only closes his other hand over ours, offering me more comfort.

"The only good thing is that your mother wouldn't have had time to tell Erica before she died either," Connor says, shrugging. "It's likely why she made sure to kill any other heirs, so that the test isn't needed, and she would be crowned without it."

"So, you think I need to hold off on killing her and do it the right way?" I sum up the whole conversation.

"Yes. The Protectors need to learn who you are, not just the rumours and the fear. A little fear is needed to rule, but without the love of the people, you will fail."

"Remember, they love Erica. They have lost two beloved princesses and do not know what Erica did. No one would believe us if we told them, so instead, we need to make them see you. You are brave, strong, stunning, and every bit of you is the queen we all need. Let them see that as you complete the tests and take your throne," Trex says, his voice commanding and his words echoing around my mind.

"We do this your way, but when this is over, and I have the crown, Erica is going to die," I warn them. It isn't going to be a quick death either. My sister and I need a family chat.

"Agreed. Trust me, I want to help you with that," Trex growls and looks between the other Protectors. "Now we need a keeper."

"What about keeper Grey? He came to us and clearly knew shit about Evie's past," Nix suggests and looks at me. "He claimed to know who your father was too."

"I met my father already," I wave my other hand dismissively, really wanting to avoid this talk.

"How? What did you do when you found out who he was to you?" Nix asks, and all the guys lean in to listen.

"I punched the idiot. Now, I don't want to talk about it. Where can we find this keeper?" I ask, changing the subject and smiling at the grin on Connor's face.

"Meeting your father for the first time and you punch him. God, you're amazing," he chuckles and so do the other guys as my cheeks go a little red.

"Back to the keeper…" I say, wanting the subject changed as soon as possible.

"We need to break into the Protectors' city and

kidnap him. I have a good idea of a secret way in, but it's going to be pure luck if we don't find trouble. I suggest we go tomorrow night as Sunday is their day off to worship in private. Most stay to their rooms, and it is our best chance," Connor says and we all agree.

"I will go and get the things we need for a kidnap. And some new clothes that are more suitable," Azi stands up off the sofa and calls a portal. I look down at Connor's massive shirt and shorts I have changed into. At least it's a step up from the white dress from Hell.

"I'm coming with you," Trex states, and no one disagrees with his tone.

"Don't forget some stuff for me! And some pork steaks for Star, they are her favourite!" Hali shouts over, and Azi laughs as he steps through the portal.

"No problem, kid," I hear him say, and I watch Trex as he steps into the portal and disappears into flames.

Chapter Fifteen

EVIE

"SHE LOOKS EXHAUSTED," Connor softly says as he picks up Hali's tablet off her lap and rests it on the floor next to my feet. I stroke a braid of Hali's hair away from her face as I slide off the sofa and let her lie down. Connor offers me a red blanket, which I cover her up with before nodding my head towards the back of the house. Azi, Trex and Nix have separated guard duties, and Nix took Star outside with him for a walk. I grab the remote, turning off the Catfish episode we were watching while Hali showed me photos of what she has been doing since I was gone.

"Hali told me she didn't want to fall asleep in case I left again, but I knew she would eventually drift off," I whisper, stopping by the row of doors we get to and not having a clue which one I should go into or where I'm going to sleep tonight. I know the bathroom is the middle one, and I've seen Hali coming in and out of the far-right door.

"I know what she is feeling," Connor mumbles under his breath and opens the door next to me. "This is going to sound like a shit pick up line, but do you want to sleep in my bed tonight? I'm not asking for anything other than being near you." His soft-spoken words make my heart pound in my chest as I stare up at him. I don't do romance, but this is Connor, the Protector who seems dead set on charming his way into my heart. I can't help but run my eyes over him and feel like he must have spent time working out as his arms and chest seem bigger than I remember. His snug blue shirt show-cases his body, making me feel like I need to run my hands all over him. When I make my way past his chiselled jawline and his killer smile to his gold eyes, we seem to just lock into this moment that neither one of us wants to break.

"Only if you don't mind the fact I talk in my sleep," I joke, trying to break the tension between us that I really don't know how to deal with. Give me any weapon, any opponent, and I will work it out, but feelings? No, I don't get how to deal with those, and they scare the crap out of me. Hali scares me, and she always did. I worried when I got close to her that I might lose her, and it made me as over-protective as I am now.

"Oh, I already know you do," he says, and thankfully walks in the room. I follow after him, shutting the door behind me as he turns on a small bedside lamp. The light reveals a small double bed with black sheets and a wardrobe. There isn't anything else in here, and the small room just adds to the tension between us as we end up staring at each other again. Thankfully he carries on his earlier sentence. "When we were in Hell, you talked for ten minutes straight about bacon when you were sleeping one night. You even made Trex smile."

"Bacon is life," I shrug, and he flashes me an amused grin.

"One day, I hope you look at me the way you do bacon," he remarks, and I don't move as he walks over to me and gently lifts my hand up to his lips. Connor places a sweet kiss on the back of my hand, the brief brush of his lips sending goose bumps through me.

"Connor," I warn.

"We don't know each other well, and there is a lot going on. I know that you don't let people get close to you, and it isn't going to be easy to get you to trust me. I wish I could take you on a date, make you fall for me that way. Or in bed. One or the other, but either way, you would be mine. I can't do that right now, but damn I need you to know you're what I want," he tells me, each sentence seeming to somehow break down whatever barrier I have put up between him and me.

"I don't really know how to do relationships. My only one ended with me sending him to Hell, and to be honest, you scare me." Connor steps back as he drops my hand, visual pain etching over his features. I step closer to him, placing my hand on his chest and feeling his fast beating heart under my palm. I know he needs me close. "You scare me because you make me feel something, and you're right, we don't know each other that well. I keep people away to keep myself safe, and because it is all I've ever known."

"Let's change that then. I'm not giving up on you, Blue. I know everything is complicated, and it will only get worse in the Protectors. They will never allow me to be with you because of who my father is and they think I'm trash. If they accept you as a royal, this will have to be a secret for your sake, but I don't care. I can't give up on us for anything, I think we could have something amazing," Connor suggests and steps away, rubbing his jaw as I try to process his statement. I watch in fascination as he pulls his boots, socks and shirt off. I end up staring like a love-sick puppy at the 'v' dip that looks lick-able and all the way up to his sculpted chest. I spot his rune name marked across his heart, and I know why he took his shirt off.

"Come and read it. Please, Blue," Connor asks carefully, and I stare speechless. Even I know showing someone your rune name means they can always find you. It gives them control over you, and it is meant to be a very private thing. I never cared about leaving my rune mark on my enemies' bodies for protectors to find, because I knew that's how they always found me anyway.

"I can't," I whisper, not wanting to reject him.

"I trust you completely, Evie. I want you to know," he insists, and I blow out a breath, nodding in agreement. I slowly walk over to him, each step making the room feel like it is drowning me in the tension between us. When I'm close enough, I trace my fingers across the symbols, and feel his warm breath moving my hair as he looks down at me. Symbols mean nothing more than drawings to me as I can't read them.

"No, I mean I can't read runes. My friend tried to get me a runes book once, but Protectors found the copy and took it before she could buy it from the trader. It's impossible to learn when you're not brought up with them," I say. This is why I know so little of Protectors, why no one knows much about them. Everything is kept in the dark, and it makes it impossible for me to learn their ways. Like reading their language, for example.

"Well, I know what book I'm stealing from the Protectors when I'm there next. For now, let me whisper it to you," he says and reaches out, pushing my hair over my shoulder. His arm sneaks around my waist, pulling my body against his, and his lips rest near my ear. My hands land on his bare chest, feeling the smooth, warm skin. *I must not lick him no matter how much his chest seems to ask for it.*

"If you tell me yours, will you read mine? I've never known…" I drift off, because it's hard to admit it and ask him to tell me something so private.

"Yes," he agrees. "But first you need to know mine. My rune name is Uruz. It means I will have strength and speed." I smile, knowing his rune name is clearly right and must have a similar power as witches' marks.

"Thank you," I whisper back, my voice drifting off at the end. He moves away only slightly to look down at me, his lips pulled up in a happy smile.

"Where is your rune name?" he asks, his voice a little gravellier than before, and I damn well like it.

"On my lower back," I say and turn around. I keep still as he pushes my tank shirt up, revealing my rune name that is written near my bum. His fingers gently trace the symbols, the simple touch sending shivers of pleasure through me. I know I need to get laid, because this reaction to his simple touches is not cool. I almost sigh in relief as he lets my top fall back down. Connor walks around me and rests his hands on my shoulders, his thumbs rubbing comforting circles. *Oh god, more sexy-ass touching.*

"Your rune name is Ashkin. It means strength, loyalty, passion and leadership," he says, and looks overly happy and somewhat shocked about this.

"Why do you look so shocked?" I ask.

"I can't tell you why, but you will know soon. Some things are out of our control, I just didn't know it until I saw your rune name," Connor says, a hidden smile on his lips as he lets me go and gets into the bed like he didn't just say something confusing and weird.

"I like to sleep on the left. It's really something I'm not willing to budge on," he eventually decides to inform me, and I chuckle.

"Even for me?" I tease, and he doesn't answer as I kick my boots off and remove my leggings and bra before getting into the bed with him. Connor pulls me towards him, pressing our bodies together as my head naturally rests on his chest.

"By the way, I like to sleep on the right. I was just messing with you," I grumble against his chest.

"I would have moved to the right if you wanted," he says. *The liar.*

"No, you wouldn't have," I call him out on it.

"You're right, Blue," he chuckles, and not much later do I fall asleep to the sound of his heavy breathing.

Chapter Sixteen

I WAKE up to the sweet smell of bacon and lying on what I can only assume is the most comfortable bed in the world. I blink my eyes open to see light golden hair right in front of me, and I quickly realise I'm lying on top of Connor as I use a hand to gently rub my eyes. *I must have climbed him like a monkey in the night or something.* I hold in a groan when I move a little and feel his hard length pressed right up against me. *Stupid female hormones making me a mess. And being surrounded by hot guys, that doesn't help one bit.* Connor grumbles in his sleep, stopping my internal thoughts, and his hands tighten on my hips. I can't help myself when I rub a little against his hard length, the pleasure rolling through me is amazing.

"If you keep doing that, I'm going to be ripping

those lacy panties off and sliding inside you. Which kind of defeats the point of us going slow," Connor protests and rolls us over, so he is lying on top of me. His blond hair is a sexy kind of messy, matching his gold eyes that are streaming with desire. He presses his length into me once more, and I moan from the intense feeling.

"Sorry, kinda not sorry. It's been a long time and I'm just…" I drift off, knowing he understands and a smirk stretches his lips up, making his sexy dimples pop out.

"Let me give you what you want, fuck, I'm dying to taste you, but it's only going to be about you. I need to know we will be much more than just once before we go further, Blue," Connor grumbles, leaning down and kissing my chest right above my breasts. I give him a single nod when he lifts his head to look up at me, and he slides under the blanket, the sound of him ripping my underwear off a second later fills the silent room. I gasp as he roughly pushes my legs apart, diving in between my legs like a starving man. His tongue swirls around my clit, and it doesn't take long before I'm moaning loudly and bucking on the bed. His one arm holds my waist down and the other slides up my chest, grabbing my right breast, his talented fingers finding my nipple. I bite my lip as the pleasure over-whelms me and everything blacks out for a second in the ecstasy. When I come back, Connor is climbing his head out of the sheets and holding himself above me. He then climbs off me to my side, pulling me against him, kissing my forehead.

"Thank you," I breathlessly mumble against his chest, which vibrates with laughter.

"You don't have to thank me, Blue. That was all my pleasure," he tells me, and I snuggle into his chest, enjoying the warmth until three loud knocks on the door interrupt our silence.

"One minute," I shout, climbing out of bed, and Connor just puts his hands behind his head, not having a care in the world. I pick my leggings up off the floor, slip them on and straighten my tank top before cracking the door open a bit. Trex is stood outside the door, his arms crossed, and his eyes narrowed into angry slits.

"Training in the basement. Ten minutes," he bites out and storms off out of sight. I shut the door with a sigh, and go to sit on the bed, pulling my socks on.

"Trex never shared anything, not even weapons when we used to train," Connor says. His comment isn't random, and I know what he means and suggests. It's not uncommon for demon women to have more than one mate in their lives, and I grew up seeing it almost everywhere. Demons were, and are, hunted so much. Women demons are usually the weakest; therefore, they end up being the ones dead more often. There just weren't enough demons, so naturally women ended up with more than one demon interested in them as a mate. I turn slightly on the bed so Connor can see how serious I am as I talk.

"Trex can rather learn to share, or he doesn't get to play at all. Anyways, I get the feeling he doesn't want me," I state.

"Is sexy teacher Evie going to teach him to share?" Connor snickers.

"Something like that," I wink, and he boisterously laughs.

"Go and get him then. I will make breakfast for you when you're done, and you are wrong about Trex wanting you," he tells me.

"See, one of my guys is already well-trained," I say, and Connor's eyes widen a little at my statement. "Shit, I didn't mean to—"

"I'm one of your guys. I'm pretty sure we both know that. It was a nice shock to hear you announce it," he stops me in the middle of my speech to say. Connor stretches over the bed, pressing a gentle kiss on my lips and leaning back.

"Got it," I whisper and clear my throat, standing up and walking to the door. *This is too much feeling this early in the morning.* I wink once at Connor, who looks very pleased with himself, before leaving the bedroom. I stop off at the bathroom to freshen up and put my hair up in a tight ponytail. I walk out the bathroom and smile over at Azi, Nix and Hali sitting around watching morning tv. Azi catches my eye as I make my way to the basement. He mouths 'good luck', making me want to chuckle, but I hold it in as I open the door. *Time to see exactly how pissed off Trex is.*

Chapter Seventeen

EVIE

"YOU ARE TWO MINUTES LATE," Trex snaps at me as I get to the bottom step. I cross my arms and keep my head high as I stare him down. Trex is stood in the middle of the room on a mat, his hands wrapped in white bindings. The bright white lights glare down on him, showing the sweat dripping down his muscular arms and the way every bit of his body looks tense and strung up. Trex has shaved his hair at the sides and back of his head and trimmed the top, somehow making the already deadly attractive man sexier.

"Two minutes never killed anyone, Trexy," I say, purposely using the name I know winds him up. If he is going to pick a fight, I might as well play.

"Get in here and fight me. We need to train,

you can't be sloppy with what is coming for us. If you want to be queen, you need to be the best and strongest Protector. Which you are not right now," he states, his voice cold and lacking any emotion. I feel like we suddenly don't know each other as I maintain eye contact with him. He has thrown a wall up between us, and I know it is because of what happened with Connor, which he no doubt heard. I want to think he is jealous, that there might be something between us other than this hateful tension, but I doubt it. *Connor was wrong.*

"If I remember right," I drawl as we start to circle each other like we have fought a million times, "I won the last fight."

"I let you. Why would I kill you when I needed your help in Hell? I won't go so easy on you now, Evie," he tells me with a revengeful glint in his eyes. I chuckle, shaking my head and not believing a word of his bullshit. He runs at me, and when I spin out of the way, he impresses me by predicting the move and catching my arm. I use the pressure of his grip to fling myself around him and jump on his back. He flips me over onto the mat, effortlessly, and holds his hands on his hips as he grins down at me. I smirk and swing both my legs into his, knocking him to the ground, and jump on his back before he can roll over. I hold him down, leaning close to his ear to breathlessly whisper.

"You're too cocky, Trexy," I quip. He moves from under me so quick that I don't get a chance to stop him as I fall to the ground. I roll over only to have him pin me down on the mat with a grunt escaping his lips as I knee him in his balls. *Cheap shot, I know, but worth it to see the pain on his cocky face.*

"You drive me mad, you know that? I fucking hate how you drive me mad," he tells me, his words slightly breathless as he keeps his head close to mine. We both just stare at each other, his musky, peppermint scent taking over my senses. I look away, only to come face to face with his runes on his arms. Trex has the same as mine, but they somehow look like so much more. I want to ask about the black rune as I stare at it, but he grabs my chin with his other hand and makes me look at him.

"You were jealous. This is what this is all about," I state, knowing he is going to deny it. As suspected, he narrows his eyes, pulling back a little so he is resting his hands on either side of my head.

"I don't get jealous," he growls out, and I only raise my eyebrows as I observe his green eyes that are full of obvious denial.

"You do, and did," I point out, and he shakes

his head. He doesn't look at me, as he climbs off me and sits on the mat. I sit up and cross my legs, waiting for whatever he clearly wants to tell me. He starts harshly undoing his bindings, and I move closer, pulling his hand to my lap, and begin doing it for him. I don't know why I want to help, and I don't even look at him when he lets me.

"Connor and Nix…they are my family. You get that?" he finally says, as I undo the binding and pause, finally understanding his anger. "I have to protect them. I always have, and I always will. Family means *everything* to me."

"You think I am going to spilt your family up?" I ask quietly, understanding what he's saying without him spelling it out. I can see his point of view, relationships with more than one person don't usually work out well, and I'm not the easiest person to be around.

"I know you will. I won't let you ruin us because you decide you only want one of us in the end. Or you leave with Azi. Connor would be crushed; he can't lose anymore, and he has already left his mother in prison to save Hali for you. Connor knows Erica might use his mother against him, but he is still here for you. Nix and me…we went through a lot as kids. Fuck, even more as teenagers," he explains to me, and I can't believe I forgot what Connor told me about his mum being locked up. I sit back a little, clearing my throat with the guilt I feel. I will get Connor's mum freed. *Somehow.*

"Nix told me about what happened with your father…" I carefully say into the tense silence in the room.

"Nix doesn't remember everything. He was so young, and it was my job as the older brother to protect him…and our sister," he says, the words sounding painful and full of regret as they leave his lips.

"It was not your job to protect them, you were only a child," I argue, knowing a child cannot be expected to protect anyone from the kinds of things he must have gone through.

"The day it happened, I had been out playing football with some other Protectors. See, there was a girl I was trying to impress with my footy skills, and I didn't want Nix to come. I thought he would embarrass me," Trex humourlessly laughs. "I made him stay at home, and fuck, it's a decision I wish I could change. I was a stupid kid."

"You saved him in the end," I comment quietly, feeling his intense stare on me as I finish the bindings on his one hand and scoot across the floor a little to start his other hand.

"I walked into my once happy home, seeing my mother dead on the floor, her hands wrapped around her cut throat. There was so much blood. Nix was screaming in fear, and it took me a few moments to even notice he was there. That my father was there. I just knew my father was going to kill him too, his hand still had the dagger he used to kill my mother with as he walked over to Nix who was trying to find a way to escape the room. I saw a dagger on the floor near my mum, one she no doubt tried to save herself with. My father didn't even notice that I had stabbed him in the back, not at first. When I ran to Nix, pulling him to me, my father looked down at his chest like he could see the dagger and then back to me. The betrayal and hate in his eyes still fucking haunts me," he mutters the end part, shaking his head like he is trying to make the memory leave him.

"I understand the feeling of being haunted by your past. Everything I've done…sometimes it feels like it suffocates me," I say, opening up to him a little and feeling confused about why I even decided to tell him that. Trex doesn't reply to me, he only places his hand over mine for a brief second.

"We cannot escape the past and what we did. I sometimes wish I could redo this life, make better choices, but in the end, I know life was not given to me to be easy," he says.

"Life has never been easy. It has been a fight, and what scares me most...when the fight is over, what will I do?" I humourlessly chuckle to myself.

"My sister walked into the room, seeing our parents and me holding Nix. I grabbed her as she screamed, pulling her to me and Nix. I made a vow to myself. A vow to never let them down again. I've already failed them once when my sister died, and I won't let Nix down again," he says, going completely cold on me again. I've been pushed away somehow in the blink of a simple sentence.

"You see me as a threat," I figure.

"Nix...he is complicated. If he doesn't want to share you with Connor and Azi, he will be destroyed by you. Or worse, you decide you don't want him. I will lose him," he informs me.

"I can't make you any promises. I don't know how I feel or what I want, but you cannot tell me what to do. If you told me a year ago that I'm a goddamn princess, half angel and that I like four guys at the same time, I would have hit you with something as I laughed," I say, and to my surprise he laughs a little.

"Four?" Trex asks, somewhat softly in a gruff voice.

"You may be an asshole, but I'm coming to understand you a little better. We are pretty alike, you know?" I remark, not wanting a answer.

"I won't hurt my best friend or brother. No matter what I feel or want," he replies, his voice gone completely emotionless once again.

"Got it. I'm not them, I don't mean as much as them to you. I'm used to that feeling," I say, dropping his hand.

"You could mean everything, but this isn't just about what we want or need, Evie. My family is everything," he says, his words a whisper, but he means every single one of them. Trex doesn't stop me as I walk out the basement, hiding my emotions, and trying not to let his words affect me. *What did I expect? For them to just choose me or something?* I'm not the girl the guys choose at the end. I've always known that, and it's about time I focus on the important things. *Like revenge.*

Chapter Eighteen

EVIE

"WOW, FLIPPING HELL," Connor coughs out as I walk into the lounge and finish clipping the last dagger to my hip. I frown as I look around at everyone staring at me, and finally at Hali who comes out the kitchen with Star. Star runs to me, sitting at my side as I rub her head. I don't know how, but I swear Star has somehow gotten bigger in the last day. If she keeps growing like this, I'm going to need one hell of a massive bed for her to sleep in.

"You look like Cat Woman, you know, without the cat ears. Though you do have the coolest cat," Hali points out, and I frown at her, looking around the room at the guys who are all still staring.

"I needed something lightweight and easy to move in, so I made a portal to the local village and found this outfit in a store," I shrug, leaving out that the store was some kind of sex shop which was kinda creepy and awesome at the same time. Nix clears his throat.

"You look stunning, love," Nix states, and stands up to clip his sword onto a holder on his back. I notice that he is the only one dressed to fight, but then again Azi never dresses for a fight as he looks scary as he is. I quickly run my eyes over Nix's tight black clothes that show me his toned body, the visible tattoos on his neck and arms matching the outfit. *I have to ask him to show me his tattoos at some point.* "But we haven't discussed how to break into the Protectors' city. The ward is a massive wall and surrounds the entire city."

"Not to mention Erica will have people looking for us since we stole Hali," Connor points out. I go to ask how they managed to get Hali out, and use that way to get in, when an idea springs to mind.

"Wall? Not a dome?" I ask, tilting my head to the side as a very good plan runs through my head.

"Yes…" Trex replies with a hint of sarcasm.

"Okay. Well I only want one of you with me when I go in, and I know just how to," I say with a big happy grin. The guys all flash me questioning stares, but Azi just grins. He knows exactly what I'm thinking of.

"I am going with you," Nix states firmly, and Azi is the first one to react.

"Yeah, that is not happening," Azi growls as Trex and Connor quietly chat between themselves. "Evie is not being put in danger without me there." I walk over to Azi, sitting on the edge of his chair. I know that he is just scared to lose me again, even if the big bad demon won't say that out loud.

"You can't go. There are demon alarms which will trigger if you attempt to enter the city," Nix tells him. I place my hand on Azi's shoulder before he can argue, and I give him a warning look.

"We need the keeper, who won't likely help me with an overlord demon at my side. They are right. You can't go there with me this time, but Nix isn't a totally bad fighter. You saw him in Hell, he will be my backup," I say, and Trex coughs out a laugh in the background as I wait for Azi to agree. His eyes roam my face before looking at Nix and back to me.

"Fine," Azi replies to me, getting up off the chair and walking over to Nix, whispering something low to Nix that I can't hear before going to lean against the wall. Connor gets up and comes over, handing me a tablet as I stand up. He clicks it on to reveal a map, and Azi looks over my shoulder as he comes to my side.

"I've marked where you will need to go, but I need to know where you will be entering the city. I think this wall is—" he starts off.

"We aren't going through any wall," I comment, and wave my hand. I take the tablet off Connor, zooming back out and looking at the building we need. It is right in the middle of all the high rises, and perfect for my plan. I fixate the memory of the tower into my mind before handing it to Nix who has a rucksack on.

"How the fuck do you plan to get in then? There is nothing underground and the place is a fortress," Trex demands, looking stressed, and for some reason it makes me smile.

"Nix is going to make a portal right above that building where the keepers' homes are, and we are going to jump through it. I guess that they have alarms to stop people coming in and out with portals. We have to be high enough to avoid that. Whoever designed the Protectors' city made a major flaw by not making the walls into domes," I chuckle, and they all look a mixture of shocked and impressed. *The stuck-up Protectors have a design fault, funny that.* Even the demon undergrounds are cloaked in wards shaped like domes.

"And the landing?" Nix asks.

"I have wings, remember? We will jump together. You will just have to hold on and pray I like you enough not to drop you," I wink at him as I speak, and he gulps.

"I can't decide if you're scaring me or turning me on," Nix replies smoothly, and Connor chuckles while Azi and Trex don't look impressed. *Sigh. This is complicated.*

"Time to go," I say into the jealous, tense room and call my wings. Thank god I planned ahead and cut massive holes in the back of the suit for my wings, or that might have hurt. I know when my wings are out, besides the extra weight, as everyone in the room just stops and gapes. I clear my throat and raise an eyebrow at Nix. He nods and turns around, calling his rune and making a large portal appear. Connor walks over to me, picking up my braid in his hand and placing it on my shoulder.

"Be safe and come back, Blue," he whispers before stepping away. Trex doesn't say a word to us as we step in front of the portal, but when his eyes meet mine, I know what he wants without words.

"Get the fuck out of there if they find you, Vi.

My brothers are fucking with Erica, and I don't want them around you. Once this is over, we need to go and see Seth," Azi warns me, gaining all our attention. I nod, knowing he has a point, even if I don't partially want to see one of his brothers again. Hali gets up and runs over to me, wrapping her arms tightly around my waist.

"Don't die this time. Promise?"

"Hali, no one is taking you from me again. Never again. You are my family, and I will always fight for us to be safe. One day, I know we will be, but until then, I need you to be strong for me," I tell her, and she lets go, straightening her back and acting more like the strong girl I taught her to be.

"You're my only family too," she mutters, wiping her eyes.

"Haven't you forgotten someone?" Azi jokes, and Hali looks over at him with a pretend confused face.

"Oh yes, Star is family too," Hali states. At hearing her name called, Star lifts her head from the spot where she is sleeping on the sofa.

"Cheeky shit," Azi grumbles, and Hali laughs as I wink at her.

"We need to leave," Nix carefully says, interrupting the moment, but he has a point. We don't have all night, and this should be an easy mission. I step over to Nix and hold my hand out. He only chuckles, knocking my hand away and pulling me into his arms.

"If I'm going to literally fall for you, I'm having you closer, love," Nix whispers, his cheesy line making me chuckle. He walks us backwards to the portal, and I close my eyes as we fall through into the harsh biting air.

Chapter Nineteen

EVIE

THE SHARP WIND beats against us as we fall rapidly through the air from the portal. Nix holds on closely to me as I make my wings spread out and catch us in the wind, springing us up as I finally manage to see where we are in the dark night. The building is right below us and lit up with lights, so I can sort of aim where we need to land. I can only glide, the weight of Nix holding onto me is too much to make my wings move. *Dammit.*

"Fuck, Evie, we are going too fast," Nix shouts as we see the top of the gold building just below us. I cringe when I know I need to drop Nix and use my wings to stop me crashing.

"I'm sorry," I tell him, and then push him away from me when I know it's unlikely he will break anything with the drop. If he does, it is better only one of us is injured anyways. Nix falls through the air with a shout, and I move my wings, flying down and landing on the roof a little shakily. I pull my dagger out of a clip first and look around, seeing nothing of danger up here. There is a row of deck chairs, fake plants and crystal lights in each corner of the building.

"Thanks for checking on me first. It's real nice to know how much you care," Nix groans from the other side of the roof as he gets himself up off the floor. I run my eyes over him, seeing he is fine and I don't have to tell him to heal anything.

"You're a big boy, you don't need me to worry about you," I state, and almost say he has Trex to baby him. I really don't think it's good for Nix to be treated like he is breakable when he isn't. I understand why Trex treats him like that and lets him drink himself into a state, but I've never been one to baby anyone. Not even Hali. Nix walks over to me with an angry determined expression, and I turn away. I walk to the edge of the building, fully knowing Nix isn't going to leave this, and choosing to look over the Protector city at night. The city is breathtakingly beautiful like this. The buildings are all lit up, reflecting off the stars and the very gold colouring of them. Somehow, I know my mother must have stared at the same city as she ruled it. She knew its beauty but also its terrible secrets. I freeze when I feel Nix press his body into mine from behind, his hand coming to rest on the bars on either side of me.

"It's quite a view. All the gold and that. I still think we should tell some of my thief friends how to break in here. I bet I could make us a fortune," I joke, and he leans his head close to my right ear. Well, kind of joking. I really think that selling the Protectors' weakness can be a plan C or something on my list.

"Love, I get that my brother has likely tried to make you run from me. I get that I'm a fucking mess who gets drunk when shit goes wrong, and I know that I should leave you the fuck alone if I really care, but I won't," he tells me, his voice suggesting he really doesn't want to be telling me this. "I can't. Azi is better for you, and he is a fucking overlord demon. That says it all."

"I guess we are both too fucked up to care what is best for either of us," I comment quietly. "But if it helps, I think you and Azi both have your issues, but it doesn't take away from how good you both are."

"You're going to make me fall for you if you carry on, love," he warns me, his fingers tracing down my arm.

"I think Trex might murder me if you do," I reply, knowing Trex wouldn't take it well.

"Nah, Trex is an overprotective idiot…but I know it won't be long until he cracks and admits what you are to him," Nix says, and his slow chuckle moves my hair across my cheek.

"You don't have to worry about Trex and me. That is not happening," I laugh.

"So very beautiful, and so very clueless about those close to you," Nix says, his gravelly voice making me shiver as I break away from him.

"We have to go, got the map?" I ask, not meeting his eyes as I take in what he is saying. I look up as he pulls the tablet out of the rucksack, his whole demeanour changing as we get back to the plan at hand.

"Keeper Grey's room is two floors down. We can't take the elevator as it scans your fingerprints," Nix states and pulls his rucksack off his shoulder. "So, it is lucky I packed rope just in case. I knew my partner in crime is more of a make-it-up-on-the-spot kind of girl, and I don't think it is a good idea for you to fly anywhere. You should put the wings away, they are a tactical advantage against Erica as she won't know you have them. It isn't worth the risk of anyone seeing you and telling her what you are. I didn't like risking it when we dropped in here, but it isn't like we had parachutes lying around."

"Brilliant! I knew there was a reason I liked you," I say, knowing he has a point. Erica has the entire city of Protectors behind her, and winning won't be easy. I need every advantage I can get. I watch as Nix pulls out two circle-shaped objects I've never seen before as I make my wings disappear.

"Our advanced technology worked out how to make a rope that fits in here and is unbreakable. We keep a lot of our world a secret, but I was smart enough to steal some stuff when we got Hali out," Nix explains and hands me one of them. He walks to the edge of the building and taps the circle against the stone that overhangs.

"Whose idea was it to get Hali out?" I ask him as I watch the circle stretch out into a metal brace that attaches itself onto the stone, and a rope hangs out of the one side, with a clip to hold onto. There is another smaller rope hanging off the other side to control the fall.

"Trex. The moment we got free, we grabbed Star and your things and then left the way Erica did. It was pure luck the portal dropped us in the city. Trex stated firmly that he wasn't leaving without Hali, and we had one hell of a fight to get her. It was a tough escape, but Hali is one strong kid," he replies. I'm completely shocked that Trex of all people would choose to save Hali. I always assumed it was Connor or Nix. I look back at the rope, knowing I don't have time to think it through now.

"Impressive. If I don't become queen of this place, I'm coming back to steal the cool stuff," I comment, and Nix shakes his head at me.

"Do you even want to be queen? Like really? You hate Protectors, well other than us," he asks, and I muse over his question as I snap the rope onto the stone next to his.

"Honestly? No. I don't know how to be a queen, but I damn sure won't let Erica be one either. If my other sisters were alive, one of them should have been chosen over Erica or me. We are both messed up, angry…even ruined, but there is a big difference between us," I say and wrap the control rope around my hand and grab the clip with the other. The handle of the clip is easy to grip onto, and I give it a tug, feeling how strong the brace is.

"What do you think the difference is?" he asks, suggesting he has his own idea.

"That I won't kill for the throne. Usually the leaders that kill for it, don't deserve it or won't be any good for the people. Hali's mum was eligible for the witch throne but backed out when the current queen killed all ten of the other eligible heirs in their sleep two nights before the choosing. Hali's mum knew she couldn't go against someone like that, and only survived because she submitted to the queen before she could kill her," I explain.

"Don't you plan to kill Erica though?" he questions.

"That's not for the throne, that's not for power. That is for revenge," I point out with a grin and jump off the building.

Chapter Twenty

EVIE

"BE CAREFUL," Nix shouts, catching my arm as I zoom down the building, and he somehow manages to catch up with me even though I jumped first. "We are about to see the penthouse floor," he warns me, the loud slap of the wind in my ears making it hard to understand him. I slow down, spotting the glass windows coming into view just below our feet and pause. The glass is far too stretched out for us to go around it. I know we don't have any choice but to drop down and hope no one is looking out the window as we do. I nod once at Nix and let my clip go, falling fast past the window and stopping the rope when I'm just underneath. I swear I saw a flash of a familiar face in the room. Nix flashes me a confused look when I climb up the rope a little to see inside the room again, needing to know if I am right. I tighten my fists on the rope when I see Erica sat on a chair in the room, talking to a man with his hood up. Every part of me tenses up as I take in Erica's perfect, innocent looking expression in her gold dress. She looks every part the princess, and I feel every bit the outsider literally looking in. Nix comes up to my side, looks in and rests a hand over mine on the glass where I'm holding the rope.

"She has nothing on you. You are meant to be in there and have everything you deserve. But not if you kill Erica now. This isn't the time, so get that look off your face and let's see if we can use the situation to our benefit," he tells me, being far stricter than I ever thought he was. And he is right. Dammit. I nod to him, and he lets my hand go before pulling something out of his pocket. It looks like a little grey stone and Nix places it on the glass. Seconds later, we can hear their every word, and I grin at Nix as we listen in.

"I'm tired of the fucking games! There are no more heirs, why can I not just be crowned already?" Erica snaps, sounding very unlike the sweet princess I expected her to be like.

"Your highness, please do not get upset. It takes time to build the energy and magic the room needs to choose an heir," the keeper replies, his voice is a mixture of concerned and scared. Erica narrows her blue eyes on him, somewhat reminding me we both have our mother's eyes.

"But we won't be using the room, right?" she asks, and I smirk at her nervous expression and know I can use that against her in the future.

"It still must be prepared. It is our tradition," the keeper replies firmly. It is clear he won't budge on that.

"Fine. I am sorry, it has been a stressful time with the loss of my sisters, and I just want to start my future. Just go. You say the same as the rest of them," Erica growls out and points at the door. The keeper quickly stands up, bowing low before walking out of the room like his ass is on fire. The moment the door is closed, Erica rises up and calls a portal. I expect her to go in it, but instead a demon walks into the room. I recognise the demon as one of Azi's brothers who helped Erica in Hell. This one is bold with a massive build and a serious expression. It is odd how he looks so different than Azi. The portal disappears as Erica walks over to the demon, her hips seductively swinging from side to side. It doesn't surprise me when they kiss, but when I look away to Nix, he is shocked.

"Not long now, Cex. Once I have the throne, you can access the grove and do what we need," Erica purrs.

"It is taking too long," he growls, his hands tightening on her arms. It only seems to make her smile wider.

"I can't speed things up. I know it is annoying," Erica says, stroking a sharp nailed finger down Cex's cheek. Cex grabs her hand, harshly pushing it away and placing his other hand on her neck. He leans down close, his red eyes glowing against Erica's pale skin.

"You best not betray me, little princess. I know you like it when I get mad, but trust me, you won't like me when I am angry," he warns her, and she only smiles like a lunatic. Being that I dated an overlord demon, I know you don't want them angry. Then again, Azi would never hold me like that and hurt me. I would chop his balls off if he tried.

"I understand," she whispers, her hand sliding to start undoing his belt. I look away, lowering the rope so we are out of sight and Nix copies.

"I didn't expect that," Nix says, and I shake my head. Neither did I.

"Let's sort out one problem at a time. The next floor is where keeper Grey's room is, right?" I ask, needing to shout with the wind blowing more harshly against us, and Nix nods. We quickly rappel and slow down when we get to the glass for the next floor. Nix slides down faster than me, pausing right outside the glass and getting four little cubes out of his pocket. He attaches the cubes to the window as I look in, seeing nothing but an empty, very dark room. Once the fourth cube is attached, a line of blue fire shoots out of them, making a perfect square which Nix kicks and it falls to the floor on the other side, making a slightly loud noise. We don't waste any time jumping in the room and unclipping the rope. I hear a slight scrape of something to my right where Nix is and go to warn him, but I'm too late as a dagger is pressed against his throat.

"Who the fuck are you? And what do you want?" the man asks, his face hidden under the hood. Nix rears his head back, smacking against the man who grunts, and Nix somehow disarms his dagger at the same time. Damn, I think my guys are stronger and smarter than they look.

"Take the hood off, keeper," Nix growls out, sliding in front of me, which seems kind of pointless as I can protect myself. The keeper steps into the light and lowers his hood, as his other hand holds his bleeding nose. The keeper has short white hair and runes on his cheeks that stand out on his pale skin. His brown eyes look almost gold and seem to have a glow to them. He reminds me of Connor for a brief second. Just a much older one.

"Nix?" the keeper asks, and Nix lowers his hand with the dagger in it.

"Keeper Grey, I would like you to meet Evie," Nix says, stepping aside. Keeper Grey's eyes widen, and he steps back.

"I wouldn't try and run if I were you," I warn with a low chuckle. "I do like to play catch."

"We need to have a talk about how not to scare people…and me at the same time," Nix chuckles, and I frown at him.

"I thought that was nice? I was *warning* him. I could have just attacked and—" I'm cut off by keeper Grey clearing his throat and getting my attention.

"Evelina Ravenwood, I never thought I would see you as anything but a crying baby again," keeper Grey states, resting against the sofa arm as he wipes more blood away. Nix pulls a tissue out his pocket and hands it to the keeper as we seem to be stuck watching each other. *He knows me?*

"Why don't you tell me how *exactly* you know

me," I ask, making sure my voice is far from nice, and he nods.

"Sit down then. It is a long story, one I have tried to forget over the years," he says, and Nix grabs my hand, making me sit down, but I never take my eyes off keeper Grey. I don't trust him, and if I find out he had anything to do with my mother being killed, he is dead anyway. Nix won't be able to stop me.

Chapter Twenty-One

EVIE

"I WAS ten when you were born Evelina," he starts off, as if telling me our age difference is important somehow. That makes him thirty-five, but I don't see why he wants to tell me that. Maybe because he looks so much older.

"You can call me Evie, no one calls me Evelina," I reply.

"If you are here to see me, I know what you want, Evelina Ravenwood. You need to claim your royal name if you expect the people to see you as a royal. Names have power, so much more than you understand. Do not worry, I will teach you," he says.

"You sound a lot older than you are," I reply, not wanting to talk about my long name. It only brings back bad memories of my adoptive parents. I don't remember much of them, only little things, but the last day I was with them is stuck in my mind. I was so angry that a toy oven wasn't cooking my cookie dough quickly enough. I look back and think what a silly thing to be mad at, but the next thing I know, the whole toy oven is on fire and the rune on my arm is burning for the first time. My parents who claimed to love me, threw me out the house and locked the doors. The last thing I heard them say was, "Never come back, Evelina." I guess that is why I don't use the name.

"My mother and father were keepers who unfortunately died in a demon attack when I was eight," he carries on his story about his life, and I sigh, looking towards Nix with a frown. I'm thinking tying the keeper up and threatening him with my daggers will get me answers a lot quicker than this.

"I don't want to hear your history. We do not have time for it," Nix says. *Who is the unfriendly one now?*

"Right. Right. I am sorry, the past is sometimes hard to forget. Basically, I was kept with the other keepers and learnt my craft by being around them. I followed them everywhere, knowing I needed to pass the keeper tests, and I especially followed keeper Cadean," he says, and I tighten my hand in Nix's.

"He called the demons on my mother, didn't he?" I ask, but I know he did. The smug look on his face in the vision is etched in my mind. I bet he made Erica the way she is, or at least made her crueller than she needed to be.

"Yes. I snuck into a chamber to watch a ritual. I thought it would get me ahead in my tests…but what I heard was far worse. They spoke with a demon, told him they wanted him to attack a woman and a baby. Keeper Cadean told the demons where to find them," he says, the horror in his eyes showing me this still haunts him.

"Did you know it was the queen they spoke of?" Nix asks, guessing some things without me saying it.

"No. I decided to warn the woman because I couldn't live with knowing a baby was going to be attacked and that I knew but did nothing. So, I ran to the building at the edge of the city, one that looked in disrepair on the outside, so no one would go in it," he stops, moving his hand away from his still bleeding nose. I feel like I'm glued to his every word, desperate to know what happened. "It wasn't in disrepair on the inside, and there were dead royal guards outside the doors."

"What did you find?" I ask.

"I snuck in through a back door after moving a dead guard and climbed up the stairs. When I got to the second floor, I heard a woman scream. I pulled the door open to see a blast of blue fire that slammed me back into the hall. The holy fire was so strong that I knew someone powerful must have cast it, and I couldn't see anything but blue fire for so long. I couldn't hear anything but the sound of demons screaming. When it stopped, I pulled myself up and walked into the room to see the queen with a sword in her back, a tiny baby with blue hair in her arms," he says, his eyes expressing sympathy as I watch him.

"Fucking hell," Nix mutters.

"I ran to her, and she simply kept smiling at her baby. The queen only met my eyes once to ask me to pull the sword out of her and find her sister," he says, his hands shaking a little and feeling a lot like my emotions. I stand up, walking to the window as he keeps talking. "I pulled the sword out, tried to heal her the best I could. I grabbed a blanket and helped her wrap the baby up. She pulled the baby to her chest, pressing a kiss on her cheek. I listened to her whisper to her baby before I ran away to find her sister like she asked me to."

"What did she whisper?"

"You are everything, Evelina. My light, my soul and part of my heart. Your father is an angel, a brave and selfless one I have been in love with since I was a teenager. I chose duty over love, and in the end, I still couldn't live without him. Your father will come for you, and he may hate the price I will happily pay, but I *know* his soul is not lost. Even without me in his life, he will have you. My beautiful girl, you are made from nothing but love. Remember that always," he drifts off as I stare out the window at the golden city and try not to show any emotion at his words. Even if I feel like falling apart at the sound of them, and how familiar they sound. It's like some subconscious part of me remembers her words. In my head, I can hear them spoken from her lips, her voice a whisper and cracked with pain that is unimaginable.

"Evie?" Nix says, placing his hand on my shoulder.

"She sang a song to me, didn't she?" I whisper, somehow remembering the tune I've hummed since I was a kid. I knew the song had to come from somewhere.

"Yes," keeper Grey answers. I move Nix's hand off my shoulder and avoid his eyes as I turn around, keeping my arms crossed as I watch keeper Grey stand from the sofa.

"Will you help us? Will you help me?" I ask, fully expecting him to say no as Protectors have never been open to helping me, so I doubt keepers will. Well except for the guys, but I'm assuming they aren't like the others.

"I could not save your mother. I could not change your aunt's mind as she hid you as a baby and killed herself to make sure you were never found. I have watched the Protectors fall more and more in chaos over the years with no real ruler to command us. Our history is hidden in lies because two people fell in love and one happened to be a queen. I wish to support a new queen who will change this," keeper Grey states and stands up. He walks straight over to me and goes on his knees, holding a hand out flat so I can see the eye rune on his hand. *What kind of rune is that?* I give Nix a confused look, and he takes my hand, placing it over the top of keeper Grey's. I feel a shock shoot up my hand at the contact, and my eyes feel locked onto keeper Grey's as he talks.

"I will be your keeper. I will be your power. I

will be your guide in the darkness that shadows the crown. You are Evelina Ravenwood, and I recognise you as a true heir," he removes his hand, leaving a tingling feeling in my hand as he stands up.

"What was that?" I ask, rubbing my hand. If this keeper has done anything dodgy, I'm chopping something *dodgy* of his off.

"A blessed promise. Come to the Protectors in the morning in three days and make your announcement for the throne. I will be there and side with you. What we just did, means I will die if I break my promise to protect you as my royal," he explains.

"Sounds shit for you if you betray me," I say, making him laugh, but it dies off as I narrow my eyes on him. "Nothing any magic could do to you would be worse than me if you pull back on your promise. I'm trusting you, keeper Grey."

"We should go," Nix says, sounding somewhat jealous as he wraps an arm around my waist, and I frown up at him. Keeper Grey is somewhat ok looking, but I'm really not into the whole priest thing, and I just threatened him. I know some people like that, but yeah, not for me. Maybe it's because I said I trust keeper Grey? Does Nix not think I trust him or something? *I guess I never really told him that.*

"Time to go?" I suggest, knowing we can't really risk being here much longer than we need to, but I also know calling a portal here isn't a good idea. We can get to the ground and call a portal a few buildings away, at least that way they won't track us back to keeper Grey. I frown when keeper Grey waves a hand, a blue portal burning into existence.

"Safe travels, Evelina. This portal will take you to London, where you can find your own way, and the alarms do not go off for keeper portals. Do try not to break anything when you visit me next time," keeper Grey says and Nix laughs.

"Evie always breaks something. I swear it's built in her," he laughs out, and I hit him in the stomach. *Asshole.*

"Thank you for saving my life as a baby. If my aunt wasn't called, I would be dead. I will protect you for as long as you are loyal to me," I tell keeper Grey, and respect shines in his eyes before he bows. I turn and walk into the portal, not looking back once. In all the years I looked for my past and who I was...I never expected the truth to hurt me as much as it does.

Chapter Twenty-Two

EVIE

"THEY'RE BACK!" I hear Hali shout as I close the portal I opened after Nix jumps through. I turn around just as Star launches herself at me, smacking me onto the floor as her giant body smothers me. I push her off and she only licks my face, looking pleased with herself.

"Star, come," Trex commands, and Star huffs, but she climbs off me at his strict command. Nix offers me a hand up, and I scowl at the amused grin on his lips.

"That was a lot cuter when you were small, Star," I say, brushing off the cat hair all over me. *White cat hair and black leather do not look good together.*

"How did it go?" Connor asks, and I look over

at Hali, going to tell her to leave and she shakes her head, folding her arms as she sits on the sofa.

"I'm not a kid anymore, remember?" she sarcastically comments. "And I've always wanted to know about your past. Tell us what the keeper said, or I'm going to make you watch more Love Island with me and give all the bacon to Star."

"Fine," I groan, watching Star's ears perk up and knowing I cannot watch anymore reruns of that show that she loves. Hali has a point about not being so much of a kid anymore, and I'm really scared the damn cute cat will eat *my* bacon.

"Keeper Grey has agreed to side with Evie. We will go there in three days to make her claim in public," Nix says and Trex nods, a small smirk on his lips.

"Brilliant," Connor replies as I go and sit on the edge of the seat Hali is in. Azi walks in the room, sweat dripping off his naked chest which he rubs with a towel. *Hot damn.*

"What is brilliant?" Azi asks, stopping between the sofas. Nix jumps onto the sofa next to Connor, who shoves him to the other end. Trex leans against the window, keeping an eye out. *Always the Protector, that one.*

"The keeper agreed to the plan and that means Evie is an official princess," Hali says, and I glare at her. "Princess Evie, the badass," Hali laughs out, and some of the guys chuckle.

"Princess Evie…yeah I'm going to take a while to get used to that. I mean a princess that once shoved an entire plate of bacon in her mouth, in public, and didn't even seem to chew it," Azi says, and I turn to glare at him too.

"None of the princess crap. I'm hardly a princess yet, and even when I am, I don't want to hear you guys call me it, or one of you is going to find a snake in your bed," I warn, and they chuckle like I'm not being deadly serious.

"But being more serious, we found something else out while we were there," Nix cuts into our laughter, and I nod, taking over the conversation.

"We saw Cex, Azi's brother—" I stop when I see Azi is storming over to me. He leans down and grabs my shoulders tightly, red veins stretching from his eyes as his demon pushes to the surface.

"Who the fuck did you see?" he demands.

"Cex. He was one of your brothers that took you from Hell. He and Erica are doing the nasty, but I suspect he is using her," I quickly tell him everything, knowing that he needs to know I am okay. That his brother didn't touch me. Azi finally comes back into control and calms down. I place my hand over his on my shoulder and squeeze once, letting him know everything is okay without saying a word.

"Cex would use her and seduce her into what he wants. It is his sin," Azi says, and leans back, rubbing his face. I wonder what Cex's sin is exactly, but I doubt Azi will want to talk about it here. Azi doesn't give into his sin, but he told me once that when his demon takes over, it is all he thinks about.

"Don't you think it is about time you explain to us about your brothers?" Nix asks. "And what the hell sins are?"

"I only tell those I trust," Azi tensely points out.

"I trust them, and you trust me, right?" I ask Azi, needing him to know where I stand on this. If we can't trust these Protectors, then we can't trust anyone. I know the Protectors have their own secrets, but they saved Hali and that earns them my trust. For now, anyway. Azi seems to pause to think my question through before he starts to pace.

"I don't remember being young or being born. There was just me as a young demon, and I appeared one day on my knees in front of my parents. At least they told me that was who they were to me. We don't look like they did, but we had no one else to guide us," he starts off a story that he has never told me before. Azi stops and sits on the floor, crossing his huge legs and holding his hands out in front of him. Two balls of flames spark into life, and he shapes them as people. I remember him doing this trick for Hali once, and she loved it. Four men, and in front of them on the ground are four star-shaped objects. The flame men pick them up, holding them in the air and jumping sideways in a circle. The star shape matches a star mark that is on Azi's thigh. He always told me it was linked to his sin, but not where it came from.

"We claimed our sins and danced all night. I was the fourth brother born. Cex is the second oldest, and the most powerful brother left," he explains, and the flames fade into ash on the floor as he lowers his hands.

"What are the sins?" Trex asks.

"Our weakness. The thing we struggle to resist. We were told that if we give into our sin, then we will find our end and neither Hell nor Heaven will welcome us," he says, avoiding telling them what the sin is, but answering in a way.

"The oldest brother…he was killed, right?" Connor asks after a while.

"Yes, because he gave into his sin. Look, the truth of it, I cannot beat Cex. Not alone, or even with help. He is very powerful, very secretive, and has loyalties to no one. I haven't seen him in a very, very long time. No one has," Azi explains.

"Then what is he doing with Erica?" I ask. He can't be with the crazy bitch unless he wants something.

"Erica said she would get him into the grove," Nix reminds me.

"What is the grove?" I ask, remembering the conversation.

"Fuck no," Trex growls.

"She wouldn't," Connor says, nearly coughing on the pure shock rippling across his face.

"Guys…what is it? Why do you all look freaked out?" Hali asks.

"The grove…it is sacred to us and to be honest, only royals can enter it. Only royals have ever been inside, so we don't know what it is," Connor answers us.

"Well that doesn't help us," I huff.

"We know you go there to receive the runes that

mark the new queen or king and receive extra powers," Nix says.

"Okay, so say figuratively speaking that Erica becomes queen. How can she get Cex into the grove if only royals are allowed?" Azi asks. *He has a point that needs answering.*

"The king or queen can take up to four rune knights. The knights are given a bond to the royal, meaning they will know if she is hurt or just needs them for something. Your mother had two knights who both died in the angel war defending your mother," Connor says.

"My mother fought in the war?" I question.

"I never knew her, but my mother did. She told me stories sometimes. I will tell you them all one day, or maybe even my mum could," Connor says, and I nod, leaving it for now to focus on the problem.

"You think Erica will make Cex a knight? Can a demon even be a knight?" I ask Connor.

"As far as I know, there is nothing saying a rune knight has to be a Protector. They only need to be strong enough to survive the blessing," he answers.

"Which an overlord demon could easily do," Azi muses, and looks to me. "I've sent word to my brother, we are meeting him tomorrow, and we can find out what he knows."

"Good," I say and look towards Hali. "Hali, you are coming with us tomorrow."

"Sweet!" she says, smiling at me. She is going to hate me when she realises why I want her to come. One look around at the guys, and they know. We are going to war, and that is no place for a child.

Chapter Twenty-Three

CONNOR

"NIGHT GUYS, I'M SHATTERED," Evie says, yawning as she stands up and stretches. The stretch flashes a little sliver of her skin on her stomach, and simply that movement makes me rock hard. I causally move a cushion onto my lap and smile at her. Her long blue hair sways around her, making me want to do nothing but run my hands through it. It doesn't help that she has tiny blue shorts and a black tank top on. *Does she not get cold?*

"See you in the morning," I eventually cough out and she flashes me a puzzled look.

"Night, Vi," Azi says, stretching his legs out on the sofa now she is off it.

"Sleep well, love," Nix says, and she pats his

shoulder as she goes past. Star jumps up off the floor and follows Evie to Hali's room to sleep in there with her. Star very rarely lets Evie out of her sight now, and the odd times they aren't together is because Evie has asked Star to watch Hali. That cat is no normal cat at all.

"Shouldn't Trex be back in a minute?" Nix asks.

"Nope. He wanted to check the pass in case the snow has melted, and we can walk to the village," I answer, and sit up straight. "We need to have a talk. I've been waiting for us all to be alone."

"Let me guess, this talk is about Evie?" Nix asks, and I nod. Azi sits up on the sofa, crossing his arms and resting back.

"Spit it out then," he says.

"Evie has trust issues and a fucked-up past of people letting her down. I like her, you both like her or even possibly love her. Trex won't admit he likes her, but damn that isn't going to last long with how possessive he is."

"Then what do you suggest, Protector?" Azi asks, looking mildly curious. "I had Evie once and broke her trust. I will never risk doing that again or fucking up, and this situation is messy."

"I suggest we all take it slow with her until Trex

admits his feelings, and we have another chat with him involved. If we rush into our relationships with her, and he gets jealous, we fight and the only person that gets hurt is Evie."

"Then she will shut us all out to protect herself," Azi muses. "So, say I agree to this plan, how slow are you suggesting then?"

"As in going no further than kissing until Trex gives in," I suggest.

"Says the asshole who has already gone a lot further than that," Nix grumbles.

"Yeah, it caused big problems between Evie and Trex. He is barely talking to her now and stomping around the house like he is ready to kill something," I reply.

"We should do this. I've known Evie for a long time, and you're right. She won't react well to us all fighting. We have to fight for her trust before we can think with our dicks," Azi says and I nod. I look at Nix who throws his hands in the air.

"Fine. I know you're right, but god we need to get her some new pyjamas as those little shorts are going to make me lose my mind," he says, and I laugh with Azi.

"I feel that!"

"When we go to the Protectors, will they accept us all being with Evie? Will our relationships with her put her in more danger?" Azi asks.

"Quite simply, yes. Multiple relationships are highly frowned upon and never heard of in my people. Relationships with demons…well that's not something anyone allows," I say carefully.

"Then we should be careful with how close we are in public," Azi offers.

"I doubt Evie is going to take our new plans well," Nix says.

"That's why it needs to be a secret. At the end of the day, this is for her own good, and I don't want to scare her off," I stress.

"None of us do. Evie excels at running away from things, let's not give her any reason to leave us," Azi adds.

"I like how you call yourself part of us now. I never thought I'd have an overlord demon friend," I say, laughing as Azi scowls at me.

"I will still kill you if you piss me off."

"Sure, sure," I grin, and Nix shakes his head as he turns the tv up, and we go back to watching the movie. I get up to go to the fridge and Azi shouts over.

"Why don't you get your new friend a beer?"

"Asshole," I mutter, but I get him a beer anyways. It seems like we all want to be part of Evie's life and are willing to fight for her. Let's hope she wants us in the end.

Chapter Twenty-Four

EVIE

I FINISH EATING my bacon sandwich just as Nix comes into the lounge and looks at the tv. I immediately see his hair has been trimmed and the little beard he had grown is gone. He looks much better and hotter than I've ever seen him. He has a black shirt on, with three buttons undone to show off his tattoos. I wonder if they cover all parts of him?

"*Jurassic Park*?" Nix asks.

"Yeah it was on…and I used to love watching them with my friend. I haven't had a chance to watch the new one, but it's on my list of things to get around to," I say, turning the film off.

"Would you ever tell me her name, love?" Nix very carefully asks. I'm not sure what he expects my reaction to be. It's not that I don't want to tell him, it's just been a long time since I've spoken of her. Azi and Hali are the only ones who know the whole story, and it was hard to tell them. Though it was nice to have people remember her with me, and I liked telling Hali about her mother. Telling her stories how amazing her mum was, so she has happy memories.

"Would you tell me about your sister? And what happened to her?" I counter, and he shakes his head, holding out a hand.

"We have somewhere I want to take you to," he explains. I shrug and put the plate on the couch and get up. Nix opens a portal, and we walk through, coming out in the middle of my apartment, next to the kitchen. Nix closes the portal as I look around, seeing that nothing looks touched. Everything seems frozen from the last time I was here.

"Why?" I ask.

"You need a dress for tonight, and don't worry, Trex came here last night to make sure it was safe for you," Nix explains.

"Why would I worry? I'm not some helpless girl and Trex knows that," I comment, trying not to sound defensive, but it still comes out that way.

"Then why didn't you want to come back here

before now?" Nix asks as I run a finger over the dusty kitchen counter.

"Memories. I guess coming here makes me realise how I can never come back to this. Yes, I was in hiding, yes, I was a thief and killed to stay alive… but it was simple. There were no emotions involved, there was no haunting past I don't know how to deal with," I answer, going on a rant which I don't even know where it came from. At the end of the day, I don't know if my newfound life is going to be better than the one I had here with Hali, and that scares me. I've never been okay with change in my life, now everything is changing so fast that I can't keep up.

"I'm here to talk about it. If you need someone. You know my past with my own parents isn't good. Everything you learnt…well, it is part of you whether you like it or not," he says, and I know he is right.

"Not all of it," I say, "I know little to nothing about your sister."

"I don't—no can't—talk about it much. It was all my fault," Nix starts off and walks away from me. He goes and sits on the dusty sofa, resting his head back. I walk over to him, and I don't know what comes over me as I climb onto his lap and wrap my arms around his neck. I don't do hugs, or whatever this is, but some part of me knows he needs me close. I breathe in his minty scent and relax. Nix sighs, resting his head on my shoulder and wrapping his arms around me.

"Love, you send mixed signals," Nix warns.

"I don't know what I'm doing," I reply. "I only know that you're damn sexy and confusing all at the same time."

"Neither do I, but I'm not going anywhere while we figure this out. Well, not until the day you ask me to leave," Nix tells me, and gently kisses the top of my ear.

"I won't ask," I quietly reply.

"You might when you realise," he says, and I give him a confused look, which he only ignores.

"Your sister?" I ask, needing to change the subject, and he stares at me for a long time, just fingers trailing up and down my back before he speaks.

"Astrid was our headstrong, beautiful sister. She was fiercely protective of Trex and me," Nix states. "I always thought it was the brothers that should be the protective ones, but Astrid became our mother in a way after we lost our parents."

"Gorgeous name. It sounds like we might have gotten along," I say, making Nix chuckle.

"Yes, you would have, and caused trouble for everyone no doubt," he replies and holds me a little tighter as he carries on the story. "The keepers sent Astrid and me on a mission while Connor and Trex were taking Erica out of the city on her monthly shopping trip."

"Monthly shopping trip with guards to carry her shit? Damn, she is a spoilt brat," I say and then gently shake my head. "Sorry, I went off on a rant. Carry on."

"It's okay, Erica was always spoilt. Astrid hated her and went off on one when Trex agreed to the engagement," he tells me.

"I bet," I reply. I think I would have loved their sister.

"Anyways, back to the mission. We went to find a Protector who had phoned for help on a simple demon raid. When we got there, the Protector was dead, and we were swamped by twenty demons," he pauses. "We called for the keepers to help us, but they ignored it."

"How did you survive that?" I ask.

"We were fighting back to back, slowly killing them, but a demon stabbed me in the leg. I blasted the five near me with holy fire, then tried to defend Astrid, but there were just too many of them. Astrid called a portal as I collapsed, and she somehow fought them to keep me alive. All I remember is her carrying me to the portal, screaming as demons attacked her back, and she was blasting holy fire everywhere. I fell into the portal just as a demon ripped out her heart in front of me," he says, his body feeling so tense underneath me that all I can do is hold him tighter and press a kiss to his neck.

"Nix…" I drift off, not having a clue what to say to that. That's the last time he saw his sister, and he had to watch her die saving him. *No wonder he is a little messed up at times.*

"That last image of her, it's stuck up here, you know?" he says, tapping the side of his head.

"She saved you. That's all you need to remember. She wouldn't want you to remember her that way, she would want the happy memories. The ones full of laughter and protectiveness," I say and place my forehead against his. I wipe the few tears on his cheeks away as I whisper, "That's what I make myself remember of my friend. The good times and not the end." I just stay still as he looks at me, feeling like neither one of us knows what to say. Nix leans a little closer, and when I expect him to kiss me, he doesn't.

"What was your friend's name, love?" Nix asks me.

"Rita," I gasp out her name, even when it hurts me to say it, and he slams his lips onto mine. Nix doesn't kiss me gently, not in any kind of way. He kisses me like he never wants me to forget him, like I belong to him, and damn, I don't want to pull away. I slide my hands into his soft hair as the kiss deepens, and I lose all track of time until he pulls away.

"I can't take this further, even if I want to," he admits.

"Why?" I ask. We are both adults. Both single. *I don't get it.*

"It's complicated," he chuckles at my confused face, and then sighs. "Thank you for opening up to me," he tells me and kisses me one more time.

"I guess I could say the same to you," I reply. "We should get back though. This place isn't my home anymore, and it isn't safe."

"Got it," he grins and lifts me off him. We make quick work of grabbing clothes and things I might need over the next few weeks before making a portal back to the cabin.

"We need food, we literally only have Evie's bacon left," Connor says, coming over to us as I open the door to Hali's room and drop my bag inside. Luckily Hali has two beds in her room, so we have been sharing.

"Trex is here and Azi went off to get important weapons or something," Connor explains. "I need someone to come with me in case of trouble."

"I have to get ready, and I hate shopping. Good luck, boys," I grin, and I hear their laughs behind me as I go into the room and shut the door.

———

I pause outside the room I'm about to knock on, wondering whether I should knock or not, but thankfully the decision is made for me when the door flies open, and Trex's grumpy face is scowling down at me.

"What do you want?" he huffs, crossing his arms and leaning against the door as his eyes run over my body in this stupid tight dress.

"You know what? It doesn't matter," I say, shaking my head and deciding I can just wait for the guys to come back or Hali to finish in the shower so she can help me.

"Evie, for fuck's sake. Get in here," Trex says, grabbing my hand to stop me from walking away. I pull my hand away, crossing my arms and keeping my face neutral of emotion.

"I only wanted you to do up my dress at the back. The stupid thing is impossible to do up, and the others are out getting food and more weapons," I say, wishing I didn't have to come to this asshole for help.

"Hali?" he asks, flashing me an expression that suggests I'm trying it on with him or something. *Which I'm not.*

"In the shower. Don't worry, I'm not trying to hit on you," I grumble, knowing this was a bad idea from the start.

"Yeah, sure you're not," he laughs, and twirls his finger around in the air. I scowl at him before turning around.

"Are you going to Seth's club then? I'm assuming so with this dress on," Trex says, and I feel him tugging the bottom layer of lace into place. It only laces up to half my back, and there is a place to tie it I think. I could tell Trex this, but part of me wants to see if he gets annoyed when he runs out of lace.

"Yep. Seth lives in the club. He has an apartment right above it," I explain. It's really smart of him to do it that way, because no one is going to start trouble in his club when they know a demon overlord is literally just upstairs.

"Why does he call you 'Evie darling'? Were you and he together?" Trex asks, pulling the lace extremely tight, and I take a deep breath in before answering.

"No," I say as I laugh a little at the thought. "Azi would murder Seth if he tried anything like that."

"Good," he answers, surprising me a little bit with his possessive tone. I turn my head over my shoulder to look at him, wanting to see if he looks as possessive as he sounded, but he is focused on the lace, and ties it like a pro when he is done.

"Didn't know you had skills in doing dresses up, Trex," I muse, shivering when he runs his hands up the lace to check it's fine. At least I think that's why he did it.

"Usually I'm taking them off, not doing them up," he replies smoothly, and a wave of jealously slams into me. *What the effing hell is that? This is Trex. I don't get jealous over Trex.* I quickly turn back, avoiding eye contact with him as my thoughts run around in circles over why I feel like this about him.

"Thanks. I best go and have some food while I wait for Azi and Hali," I comment and make the mistake of meeting his green eyes. His eyes are so strange in the most stunning way. They have flakes of dark and light green, mixing together in swirls almost. I freeze when Trex steps much closer and reaches into my hair. He unclips my hair, letting it fall down over my shoulders in waves.

"I like it when your hair is down," he explains, and I don't have a clue what to say to that or why it makes my heart pound in my chest. He moves his hand back slowly, keeping the clip. "Have a good night, Evie." With that, he goes back into his room and shuts the door. *Did Trex just say something nice to me?*

"I love that dress on you!" Hali says after she walks out the bathroom, distracting me from the problem that is Trex. I run my eyes over her black jeans, black tank top and her braided hair up in a ponytail. She has a leather jacket in her hands and what I am sure is a pair of boots on her feet. When did she get into my size shoes? I don't bother asking and just smile at her.

"That was quick," I comment, expecting Hali to have taken much longer getting ready. "Did you cover your mark up with the concealer?" I ask. We can't risk anyone seeing her mark, and I don't know if Seth knows about it. It's likely he already knows who Hali is, the demon always seems to know everything, but it's better to be safe than sorry.

"Yep, I did, and I did it quick because I'm excited to get out of this cabin! This place gets boring with doing school tests on my iPad and training with the guys. Not that they even try against me because they don't want to hurt the kid," she tells me. I chuckle and walk to the kitchen, passing a purring Star on the sofa, and stroke her head as I go by. I pick out a Mars bar from the nearly empty fridge and start undoing the wrapper just as Azi's fire portal burns into existence in the middle of the living room. Another burn mark on the floor. *I sure hope Trex or whoever owns this place likes burnt wooden floors as décor.* Azi steps out the portal, carrying two gold swords and a rucksack on his back before the portal closes.

"Where have you been hiding these shiny things?" I gasp at the beauty of them. I put the Mars bar down on the side, ignoring Azi who is staring at me as he puts the weapons on the sofa.

"I'm glad I bought that dress for you. I thought you had thrown it out when we broke up," Azi muses, his tone husky and sexy as hell. I grin, running my hands down the tight black dress which is laced at the sides and at the back. I pick one of the gold swords up and flip it around in my hand, getting a feel for the weight before putting it back. It's not as good as my purple sword, and I'm really not into gold stuff. *Unless you count stealing and selling it.*

"I know you like me in black, and you did have this made for me," I eventually reply to Azi who is still running his eyes over me. I'm not going to lie about the reason I chose to wear this out of the limited dresses I have. Azi steps closer, his fingers running down the lace at the side of the dress like he can't help but touch me.

"If you two are going to be all googly eyes and gross all night, I might change my mind about going with you," Hali groans, and Azi chuckles as he turns to face her.

"No googly eyes here. I have a reputation to uphold," he jokes, and she only laughs.

"Come on then, big bad demon, let's go and see your brother," I say and call a portal. Azi winks at me before walking in, and I hold Hali's hand as we follow. I just pray Hali doesn't hate me when she realises the plan.

Chapter Twenty-Five

EVIE

THE SMELL of the demon underground slams into me when I step out the portal and see we are in a very familiar alley at the side of the club. *I hate this alley*. I stop at the sight of a demon dead on the floor right in front of us, and Azi kneels at his side, touching his fingers to the demon's red skin on his neck. There is a hole in his chest, and I turn Hali away, not wanting her to see the mess of his body. She still gasps in shock, not used to seeing death like this.

"He is dead, we should go," Azi simply states, getting up off the dirty ground and wiping his hands on his trousers. I let go of Hali for a second, leaning down, and closing the demon's eyes.

"Demons will rise," I whisper, knowing the

demon should have some respect shown and feeling like that's the right thing to do and say. I'm sure his family or friends will find him soon and bury him. I straighten up and hook my arm through Hali's, walking her away from the body.

"Come on, let's get off the streets," Azi says as he looks back to check if we are being followed and then nods his head to the street at the end of the alleyway. I tug Hali along, knowing I need to keep her close in here. I've never brought her here before, and I can't help but feeling fearful of her being outside at all. Not until she is better protected.

"Did my mum live here with you?" Hali asks, figuring it out on her own. I smile at the memories flashing through my mind of this place and Hali's mum.

"Yes. In fact, that alley was where we first met," I tell her. "Your mum couldn't leave me there, even when she must have known I would be trouble."

"Mum loved you like a kid. I guess that's why I feel like you're my sister even though you had to do the parenting for so long," she says, and I wrap an arm around her shoulder.

"You're my family. Sister or, well, whatever you want to call our relationship. I'm here for you, remember that." I tell her as we get to the entrance of the club. There is a big line of demons waiting to get in, but the bouncers hold the rope open for us when they see Azi. One of the bouncers quietly says something to Azi, who pats his shoulder.

"Have a good night," the bouncer tells us, his bright yellow eyes matching his light-yellow skin, and he narrows his eyes at Hali. I snap my fingers in his face and place a finger against my lips. He must scent that she is witch or something. Witches are extremely unpopular around here.

"Shhh, or I will end you," I say quietly, and Azi stops, staring back at us. The bouncer looks into my eyes and then to Azi, and nods. I don't look at the bouncer again, only pulling Hali closer to me as we walk into the club. The heat blasts against my skin, and the loud music nearly deafens me as Azi looks around. He seems to see something and starts pushing demons out of the way, heading right to the back of the club and to a pair of hidden stairs behind a black curtain. We walk up the stairs, where a bouncer is stood at the top, and he turns around, opening the door and letting us inside. Once the door is shut, the sound disappears, and I let go of Hali as Seth walks into the room. Seth walks over and shakes hands with Azi before coming to me.

"Evie darling, I didn't expect to see you twice in one year," he says, grinning that charming smile and offering me a hand to shake. "I don't know whether I should be worried or excited."

"Neither, I'm afraid," I say with a smirk as I slide my hand into his. He harshly pulls me to him, wrapping his arm around me and pressing a burning hand to my neck.

"I don't like seeing you and the danger you bring my brother. Nothing but trouble has followed me since I last saw you. Now why shouldn't I throw your ass out of here?" he asks. I slide a dagger out from the holder on my thigh as I lock eyes with him. The dagger was nicely hidden under my dress, and I press the tip right between his legs.

"Let me the fuck go, Seth," I warn, and he moves his hands away, letting me step back.

"I was only being friendly. No need to get all stabby," he says, holding his hands in the air like he wasn't threatening me only a second ago.

"Don't be a dick, Seth, we have serious shit to deal with," I warn him, lowering the dagger.

"And if you touch my Evie again, it won't be her dagger-filled, trigger-happy hands you need to worry about," Azi growls, and Seth tilts his head to the side to smirk at him.

"Ah I see. Never mind then. I guess you can stay, and I can listen," Seth says and winks at me. Azi sees it and starts stomping over to us but stops when Hali walks between Seth and me, holding her hand out as she speaks.

"Hello, Seth. I'm Hali. You seemed to forget I was here."

"I didn't forget. I don't like witches, kid," he comments, walking away from her, and she lowers her hand. "You are very, very lucky you are anywhere near me."

"I'm not a kid, and it's rude to walk away from someone. *Asshole*," she says, and Seth stops in his tracks, turning and rubbing his jaw as he laughs.

"Are you challenging me, little witch with no powers yet?" he laughs out.

"Only a few more years and then we can see who will win," she counters, crossing her arms.

"Hali! Just sit, will you?" I ask, grabbing her arm and walking to a sofa as she huffs. This meeting is not going to plan. Hali sits on the sofa, flashing a smug look at Seth who seems far too amused with Hali for my liking. I walk over to Seth, choosing to purposely stand blocking his view of Hali with Azi at my side.

"Drinks, anyone?" Seth asks.

"Yeah, I could do with one," Azi replies and starts pouring himself a drink.

"No, thanks," I reply, and Seth shrugs, making a whiskey and downing it before slamming his glass on the table.

"What do you want, dear brother and his crazy girlfriend?" Seth asks Azi, who finishes making his drink before answering. I would correct his crazy girlfriend statement, but it feels a little petty to do so. And I did just hold a dagger to his dick. So, I guess I can be classed as a little crazy.

"Cex has resurfaced," Azi says, and I watch Seth's reaction, which is not one of shock.

"I know. He paid me a visit, and it wasn't for a brotherly chat," Seth replies solemnly.

"Tell me what happened," Azi demands.

"Cex wanted my blood, and he used Cheri against me. I knew he would kill her if I didn't do what he wanted. I didn't have a damn fucking choice," Seth bites out.

"Is Cheri okay?" I ask. I remember his daughter well from the time I rescued her, and she can't be far off Hali's age now. Cheri has Seth's charm, but her mother is a succubus demon, and she is the image of her with pink hair and skin. I know she is going to have Seth running through hoops when she is older and boys notice her. Though I don't know who is mad enough to try and date an overlord's daughter.

"Cheri is shaken up, but it was my fault. I let her come and see her mother here when usually her mother comes to the house, he says, guilt written all over his face. "I'm keeping her in the safehouse for the rest of her life at this point," Seth growls out.

"Our mission in Hell went to shit, and they got my blood too," Azi explains what happened to us, in a very short way. I doubt Seth would believe I was killed and came back with wings. Nor do I think Azi wants to admit he recused me from a place overlords were told not to go to.

"Why would they want both your bloods?" I ask, not understanding. I guess there might be something different and interesting in their blood, but it seems like a lot of effort to go to.

"No clue, Vi," Azi answers, but Seth looks away, running his hands through his hair.

"I heard something once, but shit, I thought it was rumours or made up," Seth admits, pouring himself another drink.

"What is it?" I ask as Azi drinks his vodka.

"That strong, ancient blood mixed in with powerful magic could give someone control over black magic," Seth says, and the room goes silent as I watch Azi's reaction. *And it's not a damn good reaction.*

"Bullshit. Black magic would kill anyone that tried to use it!" Azi exclaims.

"I wouldn't lie to you," Seth says, and I actually believe the demon. He looks worried and fearful rather than hiding anything. Seth has too much to lose, like his daughter for example.

"Hold up, what does black magic do?" I ask as I have never heard of it before.

"It's a massive power boost for one. It apparently can give you the power to control souls, even control Hell and breach the layer between earth and Hell itself. You could open and close it at will. Could you imagine someone like Cex being able to open millions of portals all around the world with one single thought? Could you imagine all the souls that would kill millions if they got out?" Seth asks. "It would be Hell on earth if Cex got that power."

"The grove must be the magic he wants," I muse, connecting all the dots. That is why he is so interested in Erica; he needs the magic, and he must have the blood already.

"We can stop him...you just have to beat Erica and become queen. You would never make him a knight and his plans are ruined," Azi says. "Problem sorted."

"Then get out of here and get your throne," Seth says and pauses as he looks back at me with a smirk. "Wait, what throne?"

"The Protectors. Evie is an heir," Azi explains. *Thank god he didn't call me a princess.*

"You have one cool girlfriend, bro," Seth says, making Azi laugh. I roll my eyes and look over at Hali on the sofa, knowing I have to ask now before I back out.

"I need you to do something for me, Seth. A massive favour," I say, still watching Hali. Seth follows my gaze and turns back to me, grinning.

"I see," he muses. "I wondered why you would risk bringing the witch here."

"I need you to keep her safe. Treat her like your daughter and protect her with your life," I tell him firmly.

"In return?" he asks.

"You will be owed a debt by the queen of Protectors. Isn't that worth keeping a witch safe for a few months at the most?" I ask, knowing he will collect his price at some point or another. When I'm queen, I will be in a better position to pay him back.

"She isn't just any witch, Evie darling. The

queen of the witches wants her head and would pay a pretty price, plus…" Seth chuckles and walks closer to me, lowering his voice, "I don't want a deal with Queen Evie of the fucking Protectors."

"Don't be an asshole. I will owe you a debt if you watch her," Azi demands, grabbing Seth's arm. Seth knocks him off and looks back at me.

"Every demon I talk to whispers the old saying, "Demons will fall. Demons will rise." But more recently there is a new saying. One only a few know its meaning and everyone repeats in hope," he pauses. "Demons will survive. The Salvatore will rise."

"It's a nice saying, but what the hell does it have to do with this?" Azi asks, his eyes flashing between Seth and me because I remember the demons I saved in Hell calling me that.

"I will watch the witch for the Salvatore to owe me," Seth offers.

"Then you have a deal," I reply. "But don't even think of betraying me. I will kill everyone you care about if anything happens to her. Even if there is a hair missing on her head, I will know, so do not cross me, Seth."

"Demons always pay their debts. They always keep their promises. Are you forgetting who you grew up with while you spend all your time with Protectors now?" Seth says, laughing a little.

"I never forget my past," I say, locking eyes with Azi for a second before walking away from them both to try and explain this all to Hali. She stands up off the sofa and shakes her head as she holds a hand up. I close my mouth to hear what she wants to say.

"I know. I have to go with the demon for him to protect me," she says, her pale grey eyes surprising me with how calm she is about this. I expected her to get mad, to cry, hell, to beg me not to leave…I didn't expect this grown-up response.

"How did you know?" I ask.

"I'm not stupid or a kid anymore. I knew the moment you said I was coming with you. You are about to fight for a throne, and I'm your weakness. They have already used me against you once, and they would again," she says. "I can't fight them, and I can't help you. Therefore, I need to be out of the way."

"It won't be for long," I say, not knowing what else to tell her without lying.

"I know you will come back for me. You always do," she says, and I gently grab her arm to stop her walking away and pull her to me, holding her tightly in an embrace.

"I love you, Hali, you know that?" I whisper to her and she pulls away, walking over to Seth and Azi. She looks over her shoulder, and winks at me. For the first time, I realise how much all this has changed her, made her more grown up. I'm so proud as I stare back at her walking away.

"I know," she whispers.

Chapter Twenty-Six

EVIE

"YOU'LL LIKE MY HOUSE, and my daughter, Cheri, will find you clothes and shit that girls need," Seth says. Hali just crosses her arms, glaring at him.

"Whatever, asshole," she replies. *That's my girl.*

"You are way too much like my Evie darling," Seth says, laughing as he opens a portal. Hali hugs Azi and me before walking into the portal and not looking back once. It hurts to see her go, but I'm relieved she will be safe.

"I will protect her. Even if she calls me an asshole all the time for doing it," Seth says, a rare show of emotional understanding before he walks into the portal and it disappears. I stare at the empty space for far too long, not really knowing how to fix the worried feeling in my head and heart.

"Hali is a smart kid, and Seth is the only family I trust," Azi tries to comfort me as he puts his glass down on the side table.

"I know you trust him, and I trust you. That is the only reason I let him take her," I explain, and he flashes me a surprised look. "We should get back," I comment, not wanting to dwell on the action of me trusting Azi's judgment with the most important person in the world to me.

"No. I have a better idea. We should have some fun, relax a little. Everything is so stressful all of the time," Azi says, and links his hand in mine when he walks over. I let him lead me out of the room, past the bouncer and back into the club. The atmosphere once again numbs my senses straight away. Azi leads me right into the middle of the dancing demons and humans, pulling me against his chest. His hands find my hips, and he somehow sways them to the music. I rest my head on his chest, relaxing and enjoying the simple moment between us. Right in this moment, I can pretend we are just two regular people dancing, flirting and falling for each other. We can pretend the world isn't out to chase us, and we don't have a history of falling apart.

"I have always loved dancing with you," Azi

tells me, and I only just catch what he said over the loud music. I look up at him as his red eyes gaze down at me, and I don't know what changed with us, but he makes me feel safe. *Like he did once before.* And feeling safe is something I really treasure. I lean up on my tip toes, brushing my lips against his and sucking his bottom lip into my mouth, biting down very gently and loving how his red eyes glow as his hands tighten on my hips. I've always loved the rougher side to Azi when he lets go and embraces who he is under the suits and the way he wants to be more human.

"You are a tease, Vi," he tells me, sliding a hand up my back. I go to reply when a shrill, shrieking alarm blasts through the club, and the music goes off. Everyone stops what they are doing to hold their hands over their ears, but I slide my dagger out of the holder instead.

"What does it mean?" Azi shouts over the noise. I glance around at the demons who stand up and start running to the back of the club to no doubt hide.

"An attack!" I shout back and start running through the demons to get to the entrance.

"You don't run towards an attack, Vi!" I hear Azi shout behind me, but I keep running anyway, knowing he will follow me. If you don't run towards an attack, you are leaving yourself open for whoever it is to attack you. *Or that's my—likely messed up—logic.* I run up the stairs of the club, which are empty as no else seems to be running out with me. When I get outside, the street is quiet, except for the alarm blaring. Azi gets to my side as we hear two massive bangs come from our right. We run down the street and turn, finding a big crowd of demons surrounding what looks like a wall of fire, but I can't see through them. I grab the nearest demon to me and swing him around by his arm. He is skinny, and his skin feels greasy under my hands. His green glowing eyes narrow on my hand.

"Get off me, you stupid demon bitch!" the demon says, shoving me away, and Azi reacts more quickly than I can, grabbing him by his throat and lifting him in the air. Azi throws him like a rag doll all the way down the street and out of sight as he screams. The demons around us bolt away, and I shrug at Azi and move further around the crowd. I search through the demons near me, looking for a more friendly face. When I spot a familiar pink demon, I run to her and her eyes widen when she sees me.

"I remember you. I never did get to thank you

for bringing me here," the succubus demon says, and I smile tightly.

"What is going on here? I can't see through them all," I ask.

"Three Protectors turned up and some demons attacked them. We think the Protectors have finally found us, and we need to run before they raid this place. The others think they can kill the Protectors and hope no one will follow them here," she explains. My heart pounds in my chest when I wonder if the three Protectors could be my guys.

"Are the Protectors in the fire?" I ask, needing to know if they are protecting themselves or if they are too badly hurt. They wouldn't have come here unless something went seriously wrong.

"Yep! They won't be able to hold the fire up forever, and then we can get answers," she replies.

"Shit," I mutter, stepping back from her. I toss my dagger at Azi, who catches it in the air and frowns.

"What the hell are you going to do?" he asks. "We should work our way through the crowd and find out what we are dealing with."

"I'm going to go and get in the middle of whatever this is. The Protectors are likely here for me, or it might be my guys. Either way, I'm no use at the back, and demons might die if they fight them," I tell him, not waiting for his reaction as I call my wings. As soon as they appear, I fly up in the air and through the crowd. I land right in the middle of three demons and the wall of fire. I don't notice until I land how everything has gone deadly silent. The three demons lower the purple fireballs in their hands, putting them out, and looking between each other. I scan around the crowd, noticing how so many of them are whispering and gaping at me. I forgot how seeing anyone with wings might be a shock to them.

"I don't know what you are, but you need to move. We can't have Protectors left alive who know about this place," the largest of the three demons tells me, his eyes drifting over my wings.

"I am a Protector, and I lived here nearly my entire life. Should I die as well?" I shout back, my voice echoing around the silence of demons watching me. They look so confused on what to do with my answer that it is hard not to laugh. Demons kill Protectors because of who they are and the same way around. Yet, I'm literal proof that Protectors can live with demons, even fall in love with them.

"You have wings…Protectors don't have wings," I hear someone over the whispering crowd.

"I am half angel as well," I answer simply. I'm not hiding anything from them.

"Angels don't exist anymore! So, you are lying! We need to kill the Protectors!" the large demon in front of me shouts in my face. I raise an eyebrow at him as I hold my hand out, calling a ball of holy fire into existence with my rune.

"They kill demons. We kill them. Will there ever be anything other than death?" I ask, curious.

"Why do you care? You are one of them!" a random demon woman shouts.

"This Protector was the one that saved us in Hell. This Protector is the deadly assassin who is known to save any demon she can. She is the Salvatore," a woman shouts, and the crowd once again goes silent except for hushed whispers. A red-haired demon walks out the crowd and over to me, then goes down on one knee. I search her face, remembering how different she looked in Hell. The demon has clearly been eating, cleaning herself up and I'm sure protecting herself since our last meeting.

"Do not bow," I bite out, stepping closer, and offering her my hand to get up. She gently knocks my hand away.

"We bow, and you accept this sign of respect. We do not bow for just anyone, now look around at your people," she demands, not looking up at me once as she speaks, and I look around in shock. Every demon here is on their knees, their heads bowed. *Demons bow for no one, not even death itself.* All the demons stay on their knees, except Azi who is stood in the middle, his arms crossed as he stares at me. Azi walks through the crowd and stops next to the woman in front of me, before kneeling and bowing his head.

"Why are you bowing, Azi?" I ask in awe.

"The demons haven't had a Salvatore in all their history. We have never had someone on our side who wasn't one of us," he says, and looks up at me.

"Demons will rise," I whisper, and Azi stands up, shaking his head.

"Demons will survive! Salvatore will save us, and a new queen will rise!" he shouts, and the demons repeat it over and over until it is all that you can hear.

"Evie?" I turn at the small, cracked voice and see the wall of flames is gone. Connor, Trex and Nix are stood in the middle, covered in blood and bruises. Trex is leaning on a gold sword, holding my purple one in his other hand and he can barely hold his head up as blood pours from a wound near his eyebrow. Star is holding Connor up by the looks of it, as there is a lot of blood on his leg, but I can't see how bad it is through his jeans. I know all the blood on them can't be just theirs. No one would survive that. I finally look to Nix, who is holding his bleeding arm as he stares around at the demons. *They look like shit, and why do I feel sick just looking at them?* I run over to them before I can even think it through, hearing Azi quickly catching up behind me.

"What happened?" I demand, inspecting Connor first. I rip at his jeans and see a giant cut all up his leg. How he is standing is beyond me, and if he isn't healing himself, he must have used too much holy fire to keep the wall up or in the fight. I stand up and place my hands on his face. "Do you want to sit as I heal you? This is a big injury, and it is going to hurt like a bitch," I warn him, and he shakes his head. I call my healing rune and place my hands against his chest. My rune burns as it heals him, but I'm not letting go until he can at least stand. Connor bites down hard on his lip, the pain-filled grunts actually hurting my chest to hear. *Whoever did this to my guys is going to pay.*

"Erica sent Protectors after us. There were at least ten, and we are lucky Star warned us something was coming so we could get weapons," Trex says, answering my question and flashing a thankful look at Star. Star stays very still as I continue to heal Connor and sweat drips down my face.

"Best gift ever," Nix laughs low, his hand covering his arm, and he must be healing himself. I glance back at Trex and know he needs help, but I can't move, and he only shakes his head at me.

"Why didn't you go somewhere else? They could have killed you here. None of you are in a position to fight a city of demons!" I scold them as Connor places his hand over mine and pushes it away.

"I can stand now. Thank you, Blue. Go to Trex," Connor says and stands, just very shakily, but it's enough to make me believe him. I make my wings go away as I look over my guys and start to feel beyond very angry. Erica can't keep getting away with what she wants and doing what she pleases.

"We have healers that can help," the redheaded demon woman says, coming over to us as I walk to Trex. I look around at all the demons watching us and back to my guys. Trex grabs my hand as I go to place it on him and heal him.

"You need to keep your strength. I'm fine and can heal myself."

"Not one bit of you looks fine, Trex," I reply.

"I mean it, I don't need your help," he snaps, and I shake my head, stepping away. I'm pretty sure he is going to pass out any moment, and then I can heal him anyway.

"Heal them for me, and I will owe you a debt. I have somewhere I need to go," I say quietly to the demon. I look towards Azi, who sighs as he clearly overheard.

"In and out? Yeah? If you're not back here in fifteen minutes, I am coming after you, Vi," he says, just as Trex collapses to the floor. I run back to him, feeling his neck and the pulse that is there. I don't want to admit that I would be seriously pissed if the asshole died. Nix rushes to his side and starts healing him as I make myself stand up.

"Evie?" Nix asks, when I turn away from them and go to Azi, who wordlessly hands me my dagger back. I didn't want to scare the demons by flying in here with a weapon, but I do need it for where I'm going. I don't care one bit if the protectors are scared of me.

"Stay here. I don't need help with this one, well maybe just a cat's help," I grin, walking over to Star and placing my hand on her head to stroke her. "You want to help me deliver a message?" Star only pushes her head further into my hand as an answer. Star is covered in blood, but I think it will only help the Protectors see how serious I am.

"Are you sure you don't want us with you, love?" Nix asks, guessing where I am going and not looking happy about it. His voice is tired and clearly in pain, and he is still ready to fight for me. Azi goes to their side and nods once at me. He will sort them out until I'm back.

"No. I am not hiding any longer," I state firmly. "Everyone needs to damn well know who I am. No more hiding in the shadows."

"Who are you?" the demon woman asks as I make a portal appear.

"The damn fucking princess of the Protectors, and I am going to claim my throne. When I become queen, Protectors will no longer hunt innocent demons. Times are changing, and demons will survive," I say, my voice carrying along in the wind like a prayer. *And in my mind, it is a promise.*

Chapter Twenty-Seven

EVIE

THE PORTAL LANDS Star and me directly outside the room I met the keepers in last time. *The throne rooms.* Which is unfortunately guarded by Protectors who look half asleep until they realise we are here and alarms on their watches start beeping. The three guards run at me, their spears held high. Star jumps at one of them as I throw a wave of holy fire at one guard and round house kick the other that gets to me. Both of them slam into the wall, knocking their heads and collapsing. Star has knocked the other one out and is sitting on him, which makes me smirk.

"Well that was easier than expected," I say, smoothing down my dress. *Not even one rip. Score.* I pick up one of the guards by his hood, and Star runs to my side. I look up at the statue of the woman with the four runes on her arms as she bows. I never did ask what the black rune does. When the guys are better, I need to learn that one.

"Time to do this," I tell Star, needing a second before I walk forward and kick the doors open. A least ten people gasp, some scream as I walk into the room, and others run away as fast as they can. *I so want to shout, "Surprise!" but I hold off on that one.* There are hundreds of Protectors here, most standing around by the walls, and the ones in the middle back away as I walk through them. Erica is sitting on the throne at the back of the room, five keepers at her sides, their faces hidden in hoods, so I don't know if one of them is keeper Grey. Erica drops the glass of wine in her hand as she jolts back in shock, and it smashes on the gold floor, the red wine looking like blood as it spreads around her feet. Her black hair is up in an impressive bun, with curls hanging out, and her blue eyes couldn't look more shocked.

"Did you miss me?" I ask, dragging the guard by his hood across the shiny glass floor. I drop him in the middle of the room, and they all just stare, speechless. "I'll take that as a yes."

"How dare you come in here—" one of the

keepers starts to say, and I tune out his rant as I stare at Erica who hasn't taken her eyes off me. Her red nails are digging into the gold throne, her blue eyes narrowed, and every bit of her looks like she wants nothing more than to kill me. Erica stands as I say the words I know she feared I would speak.

"I am Evelina Ravenwood. Daughter of Eella Ravenwood, and I am here to make a claim to the throne," I shout. Silence follows my declaration until everyone starts shouting and demanding to know the truth. Most demand that I am lying, others seem to believe me straight away which makes me think they knew all along. There was no way some Protectors didn't see the queen and my father at times. One of the keepers walks in front of all the others, and I know from the white hair hanging out his hood who he is. Keeper Cadean lowers his hood and starts clapping his hands until there is silence in the room, and I tighten my grip on my dagger. Star growls loudly at him, and I place my hand on her head to stop her jumping at him. *Even if I would love nothing more than to see Star rip the dickhead to pieces.*

"You can't just come here and claim to be a child of our beloved queen. You have no keeper to bless you and prove your birth," keeper Cadean exclaims in a pompous voice. "Now leave. You are not welcome here."

"I bless her and recognize her birth. She is who she says she is," keeper Grey says, walking to keeper Cadean's side, and lowering his hood. Whispers break out in the crowd of Protectors as the keepers stare each other down. I smile as I watch Erica slowly lose her shit, but then she seems to gain control, plastering a big smile on her red lips. She stands up and walks over to me, stopping a few feet away.

"I lost my sisters, and I never thought I would be lucky enough to find another family member. This is truly an amazing day!" she says, her voice overly sweet and she comes closer. "Can I hug my sister?" Her question is loud, and I can't help my instant reply.

"No. You can fuck right off," I answer, and the Protectors gasp in horror. Shit, I was meant to be nice and fake. *Ah well, no going back now.*

"Don't worry, I understand you haven't had a good upbringing…and you have become, well, this. I still want to be your sister and welcome you to your home," she says, smiling sweetly once again. She is playing the crowd. The little bitch. I walk to her side, standing extremely close so only she can hear me.

"I am going to kill you," I warn her, and she keeps a smile plastered on her face as she turns to me.

"Good luck with that, sister. Whatever saved you, won't work next time." Erica walks back to the throne as keeper Grey comes to my side, placing his hand on my shoulder.

"We should leave and give the Protectors some time to plan," he suggests, and I don't miss the we in that statement. They are going to try and kill him for what he has done.

"Sure. I only have one more thing to do," I say, and lift my dagger in my hand. I pull back and throw it, and it lands in the heart of keeper Cadean. The Protectors scream as I walk over to him, his hand clutching the dagger and his mouth parted in shock.

"What have you done?! Murderer!" Erica screams, but she isn't brave enough to come near me just as I get right in front of the keeper. I lift his head with my hand, his eyes seem somewhat scared of death. *After what he did, he should be.*

"This keeper killed my mother. *Our mother.* I will

not let him live," I shout, making sure everyone hears me.

"That isn't true," Erica says, shaking her head and when I look over at her for a second, I can see she is truly shocked. *She doesn't know.*

"It is. Keeper Grey even heard the deal he made with the demons that killed Eella and nearly me as well," I reply. "I have other proof, but it isn't needed." I ignore everyone shouting and making demands that I be taken away. I lean down, pulling the dagger out of his heart and watching the life leave his eyes. The light of his soul floats out his body, flying up through the ceiling as he falls on the gold floor. I wipe the blood off my dagger on my dress and turn around.

"Let me make one thing damn clear. Anyone that attacks my family, that kills anyone I love, will have the same fate as this keeper. I protect my own, and I get their revenge. Always," I shout into the crowd, and see a few Protectors flash me a look of respect, even if most look terrified. I walk over to keeper Grey and open a portal without looking back once. Star jumps in, and I give him a quick look.

"I will stay. I am next in line to lead the keepers. The test begins soon, I look forward to seeing you there, princess Evelina Ravenwood," he says, smiling at me before bowing his head then walking over to the keepers. I don't miss how he purposely steps over keeper Cadean's body on his way.

"See you soon, dear sister," Erica calls out, again using that stupid innocent sweet tone. I don't even reply to her as I walk through the portal and go to the only place I know as home.

ERICA

"CEX, WE HAVE A PROBLEM," I whisper, keeping my voice as seductive as possible as I lay my hands on his chest. I should be terrified of the dangerous glint in his eyes when he grabs my hands and squeezes them tight as he pulls them off his chest, but it only makes me desire him more. I try to forget the determined expression on Evelina's face as she strolled in the throne room like she owned the entire city. *She owns nothing. She is nothing. I will be queen.*

"You mean the problem of your assassin sister still being alive?" he growls out, and I can barely understand his words with how angry he is. I scream in pain as he suddenly throws me across the room, and I smash into a mirror. The mirror cuts into my skin in dozens of places, and I lay still as Cex walks over to me.

"I didn't know," I bite out, fearing the look on his face as he stares down at me.

"If I didn't need you, you would be dead," Cex points out emotionlessly, and lifts me up off the ground with one hand.

"But you do need me," I cough out as he wraps his hands around my throat, and his eyes glow redder than before.

"I have a plan, a way to make sure Evelina is no threat to you becoming queen," he tells me and slides a hand down my body to my ass. He lifts me onto the dressing table behind us and steps in between my legs, still forcing my gaze up to him with a tight hand on my throat.

"What plan?" I manage to cough out.

"Do you think I can trust you?" he murmurs and laughs low.

"Yes," I whisper. "I love you. I would never betray you."

"You will be queen, and then *maybe* I can trust you," he states, making my heart pound from both fear and desire. "For now, you will do what I tell you, and we will destroy Evelina Ravenwood together."

"How? Show me something at least. I do not know how to beat her in the test," I confess, and he tilts his head to the side with an evil sneer.

"Come with me," he says suddenly and lets me go. I fall to the floor, but I quickly force myself to get up and run after Cex as he walks through a portal he makes. I sway a little when I get to the other side and feel thankful that demon portals do not knock me out anymore.

"Where are we?" I ask, looking up at the massive house which is lit up with dozens of lights. I can hear traffic in the distance, and we are stood in a garden with massive walls.

"Somewhere we can get power, and lots of it. Evelina won't be able to fight you, not after we finish our work here," Cex states and grins at me before walking straight towards the house, and I don't pause as I walk after him and see what I think is an angel fly into the sky.

Pre-order Runes of Black Magic here...

Thank you so much for reading Runes of Mortality!! A big thank you to Helayna, Meagan, Taylor, Amanda, Meg, Mads, Erin and everyone that supported me with this book!

Book three, Runes of Black Magic, is up on ***pre-order*** and there is four books in this series. There is a spin off planned also. Please keep reading for an excerpt from other books of mine, and links on where to find me for updates and teasers!

Thank you and if you have a second, a review would be amazing! They are everything to authors, even if its just a quick "I like this book.".

LINKS

Here are all my links (I love to be stalked so if you have some free time...)-

♥Join my FB Group?♥-

https://www.facebook.com/groups/BaileysPack/

♥Like my FB Page?♥-

https://www.facebook.com/gbaileyauthor/

Be my FB friend?-

https://www.facebook.com/AuthorG.Bailey

♥Add me on Twitter?♥-

https:twitter.com/gbaileyauthor

Check out my website?-

www.gbaileyauthor.com

🤍Follow me on Amazon?🤍-

http://amzn.to/2oV9PF5

🖤Sign up for my Newsletter?🖤-

https://landing.mailerlite.com/webforms/landing/a1f2v0

(Her Guardians Series spinoff)

Adelaide's Fate (Coming soon)

Saved by Pirates Series (Complete)-

Escape the sea (Book One)

Love the sea (Book Two)

Save the Sea (Book Three)

One Night series-

Strip for me (Book one)

Live for Me (Coming soon)

The Marked Series (Co-written with Cece Rose)-

Marked by Power (Book one)

Marked by Pain (Book two)

Marked by Destruction (Book Three)

The Forest Pack series-

Run Little Wolf- (Book One)

Run Little Bear- (Book Two)

Protected by Dragons series-

Wings of Ice- (Book One)

Wings of Fire (Book Two)

Wings of Spirit (Book Three)

Wings of Fate (Coming soon)

EXCERPT FROM WINTER'S GUARDIAN

"So, class, please start by reading page thirty-two in your books," the professor goes on, as my class starts after he walks in. The professor looks as ancient as the old room, we are all sitting in, with his brown hair and beard, and very dated clothes–which look like he hasn't washed them in a while. I push my own out-of-control, wavy brown hair over my shoulder, wishing I had tied it up this morning. It's a hot day, and the room is stuffy because of the lack of opened windows, making my hair stick to the back of my head. I glance over at my best friend, Alex, who has her head on her desk, lightly snoring. I chuckle before kicking her leg and waking her up. She moves her waist-length straight red hair off her face to glare at me. "I was resting, Win," she mutters, hiding her eyes with her arm and huffing at me.

"The professor is here," I giggle, trying to whisper to her as she nearly falls off the side of the desk, while half asleep.

"Oh, what page?" She yawns, looking like she is going to drop back off to sleep already. I sigh, remembering how she actually has a boyfriend to keep her up all night. I, on the other hand, can't find a good one. The last time I had a boyfriend was over a year ago, and I found out he had a bad habit of sleeping around at parties. The unfortunate way I found this out was when I walked into his bedroom at his party, to find him in bed with two other girls. Let's just say he has put me off men for life, or at least, for a while.

"Thirty-two," I roll my eyes at her grin.

"I might nap instead, I had a long night," she winks.

"Don't rub it in," I groan.

"Well, you're coming to Drake's party this weekend, and no, you don't have a choice. I bought you a dress, and I found you a date," she grins. I don't know which one was worse about that sentence. The fact she has bought me a dress, which I know will be way too slutty for my style, or the unlucky guy she has found for me. I decide to go with the second problem first.

"A date? You know I don't date," I hiss, while she continues to grin.

"Hey, you can't judge every man because of one. This guy is nice, a friend of Drake's." She makes that annoying face she knows I haven't ever been able to say no to since we were eight. I will never forget when I first met Alex. My mum had taken me to get an ice cream from the local ice cream van. Alex had just gotten hers in front of me, and I decided to get the same because her ice cream looked good. When the truck left, Alex tripped and dropped hers. My mum and I rushed over as she cried her eyes out over her ice cream. I offered to share mine and then, when I saw her at school the next day, we were inseparable.

"Fine, but if this doesn't go well I'm blaming you," I laugh.

"Winter Masters, is there something wrong?" my professor asks, causing the whole class to look at me. I can hear Alex's quiet snort as I answer.

"No, sir. We were just discussing the work," I say with red cheeks. The professor raises his bushy eyebrows at me. I know he doesn't believe me.

Damn, I wouldn't believe me, either. *I'm a terrible liar.*

"Well, discuss it more quietly next time, I'm sure the whole class doesn't want to know about your dating life," he replies. I hold in the urge to hide under the table at his blunt reply. A guy about my age puts his hand up at the front, drawing the whole room's attention to him. The boy has messy brown hair that's covered up with a backwards cap. He is quite muscular under his top and shorts from what I can see. I've heard a few comments about how attractive he is, which he definitely is, but I can't remember his name.

"I would like to know, sir," he says loudly before winking at me over his shoulder. I know I'm redder than a tomato now, and one glance at Alex shows how funny she thinks this is. I'm leaving her to sleep through the class next time.

"That's enough, Harris. All of you get back to work. I am running tests on this next week." He picks up a large pile of papers, most likely the tests he made us do last week, and hasn't bothered to mark yet. I watch as he goes to his desk and pulls out his phone. I'm sure he is playing some game by the way he is typing, but he definitely isn't marking the tests.

"Also, while I remember, you need to find work experience in the next week or you'll be helping me sort out the university lost-and-found . . . for four weeks." I swear the old professor even smirked, but I didn't see him do it. I bet they would be getting him more coffees than they would be doing anything else.

"Have you heard back from the local vets yet?" Alex asks, opening her book as everyone else starts reading quietly.

"Yes, they called yesterday, and I'm all sorted." I grin, remembering jumping up and down in happiness after the call. I had applied months ago, and no one from our course was accepted, but I held out hope as I hadn't been rejected. My back-up was to work at a local farm, with half our class. Studying to become a vet is hard work, and there isn't much work experience available. This is an English class, and we have to pass it to stay at the university. That's why Alex, who is a music student, is taking this class with me.

"That's great," she smiles widely, making a few guys next to us turn to look at her. Alex is that very pretty girl you always wanted to be. She is tall with boobs and hips that are perfect no matter what she eats. I look at a McDonald's meal, and my ass gets bigger. I've been told I'm pretty, but I like my food too much. So, I have curves, unlike my skinny-ass best friend. My best qualities are my shiny brown hair and blue eyes, which I have to admit, suit my golden complexion. We don't say any more and get on with our work. At the end of class, I hand in my permission forms for the work experience, before finding Alex with her boyfriend, Drake, outside class.

"Hey, do you still need a lift?" I ask when I get close to them.

"Nope, thanks, honey. I'm going to Drake's, but I will see you tomorrow to get ready for the party." She winks, leaning against Drake. Drake is a good-looking guy, but is kind of strange-looking, and I can't put my finger on why. Honestly, he looks like a typical, scary-ass man all the time. I don't think he has a non-serious expression. He has dark, nearly black eyes and black hair that's cut in a buzz cut, but he makes it work. It's the eyes that give him the strangeness, they are too dark, darker than I have ever seen anyone's. I always thought that he must spend a lot of time in a gym or something because he is all muscles, wearing expensive clothes. Alex has told me he is well off, but I knew that anyway from the car he drives and the designer clothes he wears. It's not just the looks and money, it's more how much older he acts, when he must be around twenty, like us. Alex doesn't answer many questions about him, but they have dated a while, so I'm guessing she really likes him.

"My friend is looking forward to your date," Drake says coldly in a slight Russian accent. Alex says he not actually from there, but his parents were, apparently.

"Me, too," I lie and frown at Alex's chuckle.

"I love you, Win, never change," she says to me, as she gives me a hug before we wave goodbye. Drake doesn't say anything else, but that's normal.

I click my old red Rover open before sliding in. My mum bought it for me as a going away present, and I love the old car, though maybe not the unusual stain on the driver seat I can't seem to get rid of; I think it's red pen. *Well, I'm hoping it is anyway.* We never had a lot of money when I was growing up as it was just me and mum. As I drive home, I try to think about ways to get out of this date, but eventually come to the conclusion that it couldn't go that badly. *Right?*

"You're joking, right? I can't wear this." I gesture to the tight red dress I'm wearing. My hair is up in a messy bun with a few wavy strands around my face. My makeup is perfectly done, thanks to Alex, but I have to admit I don't look anything like myself.

"You look hot, Win," she says, pretending to cool herself down by waving her hand at her face. I look back to the mirror and glance down at the dress. It stops around mid-thigh and has a slit down the middle at the front, stopping just before my underwear, and making it impossible to wear a bra. Not that I'm worried, I'm not big chested enough to really have an issue.

"He is going to think I'm easy if I'm wearing this," I say, sighing and turning around with my arms around my waist.

"No, he is going to think he is a lucky fucker," she laughs before straightening her own dress. Alex is wearing her little black dress, which is a little too little but looks nice.

"Alright. But again, I'm blaming you if anything goes wrong." I laugh to myself, knowing this could only go wrong. I shut the door to my bedroom before leaving our apartment. Alex and I have a two-bedroom apartment near the university, which we rent together. It's cheap enough, and the area isn't too bad, but we still make sure we lock up.

"So, what's my date's name?" I ask as we wait outside for Drake to turn up. We are lucky the weather has been so good recently. Welsh weather is known for its constant rain, and our town is right in the middle of the mountains. Calroh is a small town but has a great university, and that's why we chose it, also the cheap apartments to rent helped. It's right in the middle of two large mountains and surrounded by a large forest. There's only one road out of town, but the town is well-stocked enough to look after itself with many large superstores.

"Wyatt. I haven't met him, but Drake speaks highly of him." She winks at me.

I think of his name for a second, trying to imagine the guy. "So, is it getting serious between you and Drake?" I ask gently, knowing Alex doesn't like to speak about relationships. Not her own at least.

"I don't know. He is so secretive that I–" she stops talking as Drake's car pulls in front us. I glance at her, and I am wondering what the end of that sentence was, but she shakes her head, smiling before opening her door. I do the same sliding into the back.

"Hey, Drake," I say as I get in, and Alex pulls back from kissing Drake hello.

"I thought Wyatt was coming with us?" Alex asks, noticing the empty seat by me. I smile widely, hoping he is ill or isn't coming.

"He is meeting us there," Drake says bluntly before driving off.

There goes my dream of taking off this dress and changing into my PJ's, with a bottle of wine.

I don't say anything, growing a little more nervous the nearer we get to Drake's apartment.

As we pull into the expensive apartment building, we can see the party has started. The music is loud, and there are cars everywhere. I mentally tell myself that going to a party at twenty years old is normal, and I should smile before getting out of the car. I walk next to Alex as Drake puts his arm around her shoulders. Just as we walk in, and the loud music fills my ears, I see a blond man leaning against the wall next to the door of Drake's apartment. I can't help but stare a little at his muscular frame and his strong-looking face that I have to admit is a little scary. He seems to notice me staring and looks right at me. I first notice his eyes are that nearly black in colour or maybe just a dark-brown like Drake's. I look around quickly noticing that nearly every girl nearby is watching the breathtaking guy like I am. My eyes draw back to his, noticing how powerful he looks. He can't be more than twenty-five but looks like he owns the very street he is standing on. The guy's eyes never leave mine as I look him over, and I shiver from the anger I feel in his eyes. *How can someone look so serious and cold at our age?* I continue walking with Alex until we stop in front of the guy, and I want to get to know him or hear him speak. My mind and body feel drawn to him, and I don't like it.

"Drake, this must be my date," the man says in a dark, underwear-dropping voice, nodding at Drake before looking back at me. I feel myself blush as his gaze takes in all of me slowly. I do the same, noticing for the first time that he is wearing a black jumper with black jeans, which look like they were custom-made for him; they possibly were.

"Wyatt. It's nice to meet you, Winter," he offers his hand. I take his cold hand, and he shocks me by bringing it up to his mouth and placing a kiss on the back. His lips feel cold on my hand, but I feel a strange shock when his lips meet my skin. It takes everything in me not to pull my hand away and run in the other direction like my body is screaming for me to do. For some reason, I don't feel safe with him.

"Nice to meet you, too," I mutter a slight lie, pulling back my hand.

Wyatt just flashes me a knowing look before saying to Drake, "There was a problem tonight, they are getting braver," his deep voice gets stronger about whatever they are discussing. It's almost like his voice draws you in and demands that you listen.

"Just a few newbies chasing a pup, it's being dealt with," Drake smiles with a cold look in my direction.

"Good. Now, can I get you a drink?" Wyatt asks looking back at me. It's strange to see how Wyatt spoke to Drake then. It was like a boss ordering around an employee, and worse, I had no idea what they were speaking about. *What's a pup?* Maybe it's a kind of business talk, I doubt they mean a puppy.

"Sure," I say taking his open arm and letting him guide me through the house. I can feel how cold he is even through his jacket. I look back to see Alex, who has disappeared with Drake. Knowing Alex, they might have already left, thinking Wyatt seems nice. I don't feel that he is at all; he seems too haunted to be described as nice. Seeing how he spoke to Drake just then, makes me more distrusting of him.

"Are you cold?" I ask noticing that's it's a hot summer day in May. I'm even warm, in a little dress, and he is cold in a jumper.

"Just cold-blooded," he winks at me. I can't help but blush a little, but who wouldn't when a very hot guy flirts with you. I know I need to act normal for a bit, before making an excuse and leaving. We weave through the hallways of the building and up two floors in the elevator, which is filled with couples making out. I watch as they stop and stare at Wyatt like he is a god and ignore me completely. It's all very odd.

"So, tell me, what do you study?" he asks as we enter the kitchen. It's a modern kitchen with many cabinets that don't look used, and there's even a bar on the one side next to an impressive window. There are a few people around, but it's quiet enough in here to not have to talk too loudly. Wherever the loud music is coming from, it's not nearby.

"I'm studying to become a vet. What about you?" I look over the view of the nearby forest and mountains as he hands me an opened beer. I don't like beer, but I'm not telling him that, so I pretend to drink it.

"The family business," he says still looking at me. He moves closer, so I have to lift my head up to look at him.

Being so short can be really an annoying at times, I think to myself. This guy has at least a foot on me, and I feel small around him. Now that he is closer, I can see that his eyes are definitely black with little silver sparks in them. I've never seen eyes like his, and they are really stunning. I clear my throat before asking, "Have you known Drake long?"

"Yes, it feels like I've known Drake forever sometimes," he grins at me like I'm missing a joke.

"I feel like that with Alex sometimes," I say, looking away because his eyes are so stunning that they draw you in. The other door in the room opens as a drunken man stumbles in, he quickly leaves again when he sees Wyatt but leaves the door open. I can see the living room, well it's more a dance room. The dancing bodies are pushed so closely together that you can't see their faces. The music is beating hard and fast compared to the slow-moving young people swaying around. I turn back to see Wyatt watching me closely.

"Dance with me? You seem like you need to relax," he asks. I lift my head to stare into his eyes, and I feel the need to dance with him, to do anything he wants. I stare at his eyes as he smirks, moving closer to me. I could have sworn his eyes had silver sparks, nothing like the empty, black pits I'm staring into now.

I shake my head, stepping back. "No thanks, I don't dance," I say to Wyatt's cold gaze. This time, his face converts into confusion, and he steps closer to me than before. We are almost touching with how close he is.

"Dance with me, Winter," he says looking into my eyes again, his eyes glowing far brighter than they should. I yelp when he grabs my arm roughly. I take a step away. His grip is strong, but I realise he isn't trying to hurt me. I don't dare look away from him as the black, glowing eyes stare into me, like he is looking into my soul.

"No, let go, Wyatt," I say firmly, challenging his

grip by struggling away. I don't know what changes, but he lets me go with an utterly confused and shocked look marking his handsome face.

"How is that possible?" he mutters to himself, running his hands through his hair, and stepping away from me. I take the chance he gives me to run out the door, not caring who is looking. I have a feeling challenging a scary man like that is not a good idea. I don't think running from him is a good idea either, but, hey, it's all I have right now. *I couldn't have seen glowing eyes, right?* I mean that doesn't even make sense to me, it must have been a trick of the light or something. I eventually make my way outside. I can't believe my luck when I spot the guy from class, Harris, opening his car door for a young girl to get in. I'm glad I remembered his name now.

"Wait, Harris!" I shout from the door, and he turns to me, looking a little shocked, but more worried than anything else.

"Are you alright?" he asks none too gently as he grabs my shoulders, pulling me closer, and looking me up and down.

"Yes, but I could use a lift home," I say gently as I pull away from him a little, enough that he drops his warm hands.

"Sure, I was just taking my sister home. My

parents are going to kill her for sneaking out tonight. So, I'm sure she needs some extra time to come up with a decent excuse," he laughs, opening the back door for me.

As I get in, I look behind me to see Wyatt watching me from the door. I swear I'll never forget the look he has on his face as watches me get into the car. He is looking at me like he is a starving man, and I am his meal. I gasp before slamming the door shut and closing my eyes for a second, resting my head against the cold leather.

"So, what's your name?" the girl in the front asks the minute I get in. I smile as I hear her draw out the sentence. I open my eyes to see a pair of light-blue ones sparkling at me.

"I'm Winter, and you are?" I put on my seat belt as Harris gets in.

"I'm Katy. How do you know my brother?" she smiles, but it looks cheeky.

"You should be thinking of excuses to help yourself, and not asking questions," Harris answers her question as he looks at me in the rear-view mirror. I smirk at him when I see he is trying not to laugh, and he winks at me.

"They are going to ground me for life, anyway," she says to Harris with a huff and looks back at me, "so, do you have a boyfriend?" she asks, clearly not concerned about her parents, and I look her over now. She has the same light-brown hair as Harris and matching blue eyes, that are lighter than most. I would guess she is around sixteen, making her way too young to be here. She is wearing a purple dress that is as short as mine but makes her look a hell of a lot older than she is. I can see why Harris' parents are going to be mad. I'm guessing the amount of makeup she has on isn't going to help her case. She doesn't need it, though, I can see under it all that she is very pretty.

"No. I'm escaping a bad date, actually," I mutter as she laughs.

"Harris should ask you out, he wouldn't be a bad date," she winks, and I see Harris blush.

"I'm not dating anymore, but if I was, Harris would be a good choice," I say gently, letting them both down easily.

"You should change your mind. You're really pretty." She sighs, finally turning around. Harris asks for the address, so I give it to him before opening my phone. I'm surprised not to see any messages from Alex. I send her a quick one:

Date was awful, shame the hot ones are

always crazy. I got a lift home. I will see you tomorrow. Love you xx

I missed out on the start of the argument, as I was texting, but from Harris's angry face he isn't happy.

"There are loads of them around right now, Katy. I don't want to find you sneaking out again!" he shouts, leaving me to wonder what he is talking about. Katy is looking tense in her seat at whatever it is.

"I know. But, I never get to leave the pack," she says looking out the window with a long sigh. I'm sure that I see tears in her eyes as she picks her nails, looking worried.

"It won't always be like this, but please, for me, don't leave again without one of us." He stares at her through the mirror, and I see her lower her gaze quickly.

"I promise," Katy says with a frown, and Harris nods, looking back at the empty road. I watch as he turns to look at me, and a grin lights up his face when he sees what I'm wearing. Typical guy, but at least he has the common sense to look back at the road after a second, not voicing his opinion.

"What's a pack?" I ask clearing my throat and hopefully my red cheeks from Harris's stare. I remember reading about packs of wolves in class, but I don't think they are talking about that. Maybe it's some kind of gang or a name of a house, I don't want to guess because I'm sure I'm going to come up with something worse than what it actually is. I glance at Harris who isn't answering my question, so I repeat myself.

"Oh, it's nothing important," Harris says quickly, all the while he is glaring at Katy like a parent whose kid just told someone a big secret of theirs. I glance back at Katy, who looks very guilty, as she shrugs at me, and avoids looking at Harris at all. This night is proving to be all kinds of confusing, and I'm pretty sure forgetting it is the easier way. No one says anything else while we drive home, and a tense silence descends on the car.

"Are you going to be okay to walk in? I don't think I can get in the car park with the gate down," Harris looks at me, as he stops on the road outside my building. The whole building is close to the university, so it has to be on lockdown after a certain time, and you can only walk in, past a locked gate. I'm lucky the gate's broken, so you don't need a key to get in. Well, unlucky in certain ways because it means anyone can get in.

"Yeah, I'll walk in. The gate is open," I say to

Harris, and he nods, watching me closely like he wants to say something, but I get out of the car before he can.

"Bye, Katy, and good luck with your parents," I say through the open window, and I laugh, hearing her grumble before I move away from the car. I wave them both off before opening the broken gate to the locked car park, the door is slightly open anyway from our neighbours. The car park is almost as big as the building in length, and you have to walk across the whole thing to get to my building. My building has three flats, on three levels, and we have the bottom one. The car park is empty, besides my car and one other. I walk slowly; only the dim lights of the street lamps near the building are lighting my path, showing me where I'm going. In the distance, I notice a big, dark shape lying next to my car, near the door to my building. I run over quickly, my footsteps being the only noise in the dark night. I'm hoping the person is okay and pull my phone out of my bag as I run, to call an ambulance, but as I get closer I see it's a wolf.

Could my night get any weirder?

For more information, click here.

Runes
of
Black Magic

Book Three coming soon...

Printed in Great Britain
by Amazon

66240948R00147